DAVID MOODY

GOLLANCZ

LONDON

The right of David Moody to be identified as the author
of this work has been asserted by him in accordance with
the Copyright, Designs and Patents Act 1988.

First published in Great Britain in 2009 by
Gollancz
An imprint of the Orion Publishing Group
Orion House, 5 Upper St Martin's Lane,
London WC2H 9EA
An Hachette UK Company

A CIP catalogue record for this book
is available from the British Library

ISBN 978 0 575 08466 7 (Cased)
ISBN 978 0 575 08467 4 (Trade Paperback)

1 3 5 7 9 10 8 6 4 2

Typeset at The Spartan Press Ltd,
Lymington, Hants

Printed and bound in the UK by CPI Mackays,
Chatham ME5 8TD

The Orion Publishing Group's policy is to use papers that
are natural, renewable and recyclable products and made
from wood grown in sustainable forests. The logging and
manufacturing processes are expected to conform to the
environmental regulations of the country of origin.

www.orionbooks.co.uk

THURSDAY

i

Simmons, regional manager for a chain of high street discount stores, slipped his change into his pocket then neatly folded his newspaper in half and tucked it under his arm. He quickly glanced at his watch before leaving the shop and rejoining the faceless mass of shoppers and office workers crowding the city centre pavements outside. He checked through his diary in his head as he walked. Weekly sales meeting at ten, business review with Jack Staynes at eleven, lunch with a supplier at one-thirty . . .

He stopped walking when he saw her. At first she was just another face on the street, nondescript and unimposing and as irrelevant to him as the rest of them were. But there was something different about this particular woman, something that made him feel uneasy. In a split second she was gone again, swallowed up by the crowds. He looked round for her anxiously, desperate to find her among the constantly weaving mass of figures which scurried busily around him. There she was. Through a momentary gap in the bodies he could see her coming towards him. No more than five feet tall, hunched forward and wearing a faded red raincoat. Her wiry grey-white hair was held in place under a clear plastic rain-hood and she stared ahead through the thick lenses of her wide-rimmed glasses. She had to be eighty if she was a day he thought as he looked into her wrinkled, liver-spotted face, so why was she such a threat? He had to act quickly before she disappeared again. He couldn't risk losing her. For the first time he made direct eye contact with her and he knew immediately that he had to do it. He had no choice. He had to do it and he had to do it right now.

Dropping his newspaper, briefcase and umbrella Simmons pushed his way through the crowd then reached out and grabbed hold of her by the wide lapels of her raincoat. Before she could react to what was happening he spun her round through almost a complete turn and threw her back towards the building he'd just left. Her frail body was light and she virtually flew across the footpath, her feet barely touching the ground before she smashed up against the thick safety-glass shop window and bounced back into the street. Stunned with pain and surprise she lay face down on the cold, rain-soaked pavement, too shocked to move. Simmons pushed his way back towards her, barging through a small crowd of concerned shoppers who had stopped to help. Ignoring their angry protests he dragged her to her feet and shoved her towards the shop window again, her head whipping back on her shoulders as she clattered against the glass for the second time.

'What the hell are you doing, you idiot?!' an appalled bystander yelled, grabbing hold of Simmons's coat sleeve and pulling him back. Simmons twisted and squirmed free from the man's grip. He tripped and landed on his hands and knees in the gutter. She was still on her feet just ahead of him. He could see her through the legs of the other people crowding around her.

Oblivious to the howls and screams of protest ringing in his ears, Simmons quickly stood up, pausing only to pick up his umbrella from the edge of the footpath and to push his wire-framed glasses back up the bridge of his nose. Holding the umbrella out in front of him like a bayonet rifle he ran at the woman again.

'Please . . .' she begged as he sunk the sharp metal tip of the umbrella deep into her gut and then yanked it out again. She slumped back against the window, clutching the wound as the stunned and disbelieving crowd quickly engulfed Simmons. Through the confusion he watched as her legs gave way and she collapsed heavily to the ground, blood oozing out of the deep hole in her side.

'Maniac,' someone spat in his ear. Simmons spun around and stared at the owner of the voice. Jesus Christ, another one! This one was just like the old woman. And there's another, and another . . . and they were all around him now. He stared helplessly into the sea of angry faces that surrounded him. They were all the same. Every last one of them had suddenly become a threat to him. He knew there were too many of them but he had *to fight. In desperation he screwed his hand into a fist and swung it into the nearest face. As a teenage boy recoiled from the sudden impact and dropped to the ground a horde of uniformed figures weaved through the crowd and wrestled Simmons to the ground.*

1

L unatic. Bloody hell, I've seen some things happen in this town before but never anything like that. That was disgusting. That made me feel sick. Christ, he came out of nowhere and she didn't stand a chance, poor old girl. He's in the middle of the crowd now. He's outnumbered fifty-to-one and yet he's still trying to fight. This place is full of crazy people. Fortunately for that woman it's also full of police officers. There are two of them down with her now, trying to stop the bleeding. Three more have got to the bloke that did it and they're dragging him away.

Damn, it's three minutes to nine. I'm going to be late for work again but I can't move. I'm stuck in this bloody crowd. There are people bunched up tight all around me and I can't go backwards or forwards. I'll have to wait until they start to shift, however long that takes. There are more police officers arriving now trying to clear the scene. It's pathetic really, you'd think they'd show some respect but people are all the same. First sign of trouble on the street and everyone stops to watch the freak show.

We're finally starting to move. I can still see that bloke being bundled towards a police van on the other side of the street. He's kicking and screaming and crying like a bloody baby. Looks like he's lost it completely. The noise he's making you'd think he was the one who'd been attacked.

I know I'm a lazy bastard. I know I should try harder but I just can't be bothered. I'm not stupid but I sometimes find it difficult to give a shit. I should have run across Millennium Square to get to the office just now but it was too much effort so early in the morning. I walked and I finally got here at just gone quarter past nine. I tried to sneak in but it was inevitable that someone was going to see me. It had to be Tina Murray though, didn't it? My sour-faced, slave-driving, unforgiving bitch of a supervisor. She's standing behind me now, watching me work. She thinks I don't know she's there. I really can't stand her. In fact I can't think of anyone I like less than Tina. I'm not a violent man – I don't like confrontation and I find the very idea of punching a woman offensive – but there are times here when I'd happily smack her in the mouth.

'You owe me fifteen minutes,' she sneers in her horrible, whining voice. I push myself back on my chair and slowly turn around to face her. I force myself to smile although all I want to do is spit. She stands in front of me, arms folded, chewing gum and scowling.

'Morning, Tina,' I reply, trying to stay calm and not give her the satisfaction of knowing just how much she winds me up, 'how are you today?'

'You can either take the time off your lunch hour or stay back tonight and work over,' she snaps. 'It's up to you how you make it up.'

I know I'm only making things worse for myself but I can't help it. I should just keep my mouth shut and accept that I'm in the wrong but I can't stand the thought of this vile woman thinking she's in control. I know I'm not helping the situation but I just can't stop myself. I have to say something.

'What about yesterday morning?' I ask. I force myself to look into her harsh, scowling face again. She's not at all happy. She shifts her weight from one foot to the other and chews her gum even harder and faster. Her jaw moves in a frantic circular motion. She looks like a cow chewing the cud. Fucking heifer.

'What about yesterday morning?' she spits.

'Well,' I explain, trying hard not to sound like I'm patronising her, 'if you remember I was twenty minutes early yesterday and I started working as soon as I got here. If I'm going to make up your fifteen minutes for today, can I claim back my twenty minutes for yesterday? Or shall we just call it quits and I'll let you off the five minutes?'

'Don't be stupid. You know it doesn't work like that.'

'Maybe it should.'

Bloody hell, now she's really annoyed. Her face is flushed red and I can see the veins on her neck bulging. It was a stupid and pointless comment to make but I'm right, aren't I? Why should the council have it all their own way? Tina's staring at me now and her silence is making me feel really uncomfortable. I should have just kept my mouth closed. I let her win the face-off and I turn back round to sign on to my computer again.

'Either take it off your lunch hour or work over,' she says over her shoulder as she walks away. 'I don't care what you do, just make sure you make up the time you owe.'

And she's off. Conversation's over and I don't get any chance to respond or to try and get the last word. Bitch.

Tina makes my skin crawl but I find myself staring at her rather than my computer screen. She's back at her desk now and Barry Penny, the office manager, has suddenly appeared. Her body language has completely changed now that she's speaking to someone who's higher up the council pecking order than she is. She's smiling and laughing at his pathetic jokes and generally trying to see how far she can crawl up his backside.

I can't help thinking about what I've just seen happen outside. Christ, I wish I had that bloke's umbrella. I know exactly where I'd shove it.

Sometimes having such a dull and monotonous job is an advantage. This stuff is way beneath me and I don't really have to think about what I'm doing. I can do my work on autopilot and the time passes quickly. It's been like that so far this morning. Job satisfaction is non-existent but at least the day isn't dragging.

I've been working here for almost eight months now (it feels longer) and I've worked for the council for the last three and a half years. In that time I've worked my way through more departments than most long-serving council staff manage in their entire careers. I keep getting transferred. I served time in the pest control, refuse collection and street lamp maintenance departments before I ended up here in the Parking Fine Processing office or PFP as the council likes to call it. They have an irritating habit of trying to reduce as many department names and job titles down to sets of initials as they can. Before I was transferred here I'd been told that the PFP was a dumping ground for underperformers and, as soon as I arrived, I realised it was true. In most of the places I've worked I've either liked the job but not the people or the other way around. Here I have problems with both. This place is a breeding ground for trouble. This is where those motorists who've been unlucky (or stupid) enough to get wheel-clamped, caught on camera or given a ticket by a parking warden come to shout and scream and dispute their fines. I used to have sympathy with them and I believed their stories. Eight months here has changed me. Now I don't believe anything that anyone tells me.

'Did you see that bloke this morning?' a voice asks from behind the computer on my left. It's Kieran Smyth. I like Kieran. Like most of us he's wasted here. He's got brains and he could make something of himself if he tried. He was studying law at university but took a holiday job here last summer and never went back to class. Told me he got used to having the money and couldn't cope without it. He buys an incredible amount of stuff. Every day he seems to come back from lunch with bags of clothes, books, DVDs and CDs. I'm just jealous because I struggle to scrape together enough money to buy food, never mind anything else. Kieran spends most of his day talking to his mate Daryl Evans who sits on my right. They talk through me and over me but very rarely to me. It doesn't bother me though. Their conversations are as boring as hell and the only thing I have in common with them is that the three of us all work within the same small section of the same small office. What does annoy me, if I'm honest, is the fact that they both seem to be able to get away with not doing very much for large chunks of the working day. Maybe it's because they're friendly with Tina outside work and they go out drinking together. Christ, I only have to cough and she's up out of her seat wanting to know what I'm doing and why I've stopped working.

'What bloke?' Daryl shouts back.

'Out on the street on the way to work.'

'Which street?'

'The high street, just outside Cartwrights.'

'Didn't see anything.'

'You must have.'

'I didn't. I didn't walk past Cartwrights. I came the other way this morning.'

'There was this bloke,' Kieran explains regardless, 'you should have seen him. He went absolutely fucking mental.'

'What are you on about?'

'Honest mate, he was wild. You ask Bob Rawlings up in Archives. He saw it. He reckons he practically killed her.'

'Killed who?'

'I don't know, just some old woman. No word of a lie, he just started laying into her for no reason. Stabbed her with a bloody umbrella I heard!'

'Now you're taking the piss . . .'

'I'm serious.'

'No way!'

'You go and ask Bob . . .'

I usually ignore these quick-fire conversations (most of the time I don't have a clue what they're talking about) but today I can actually add something because I was there. It's pathetic, I know, but the fact that I seem to know more about what happened than either Kieran or Daryl makes me feel smug and superior.

'He's right,' I say, looking up from my screen.

'Did you see it then?' Kieran asks. I lean back on my seat in self-satisfaction.

'Happened right in front of me. He might even have gone for me if I'd been a few seconds earlier.'

'So what was it all about?' Daryl asks. 'Is what he's saying right?'

I quickly look over at Tina. She's got her head buried in a pile of papers. It's safe to keep talking.

'I saw the old girl first,' I tell them. 'I nearly tripped over her. She came flying past me and smashed up against the window by the side door of Cartwrights. I thought it must be a group of kids trying to get her bag off her or something like that. Couldn't believe it when I saw him. He just looked like a normal bloke. Suit, tie, glasses . . .'

'So why did he do it? What had she done to him?'

'No idea. Bloody hell, mood he was in I wasn't about to ask him.'

'And he just went for her?' Daryl mumbles, sounding like he doesn't believe a word I'm saying. I nod and glance from side to side at both of them.

'Never seen anything like it,' I continue. 'He ran at her and stabbed her with an umbrella. It was gross. It went right into her belly. There was blood all over her coat and . . .'

Tina's looking up now. I look down and start typing, trying to remember what it was I was doing.

'Then what?' Kieran hisses.

'Idiot turned on the rest of the crowd. Started hitting out at the people around him. Then the police turned up,' I explain, still looking at my screen but not actually doing anything. 'They dragged him away and shoved him in the back of a van.'

The conversation stops again. Murray's on the move. For a moment the only sound I can hear is the clicking of three computer keyboards as we pretend to work. After looking around the room and staring at me in particular she leaves the office and Kieran and Daryl immediately stop inputting.

'So was there something wrong with him?' Daryl asks point-lessly.

'Of course there was something wrong with him,' I answer. Christ, this bloke's an idiot at times. 'Do you think he'd stab an old lady with an umbrella if there wasn't anything wrong with him?'

'But did he say anything? Was he screaming or shouting or . . . ?'

I wonder whether it's even worth answering his half-asked question.

'Both,' I grunt.

'Was he drunk or on drugs or . . . ?'

'I don't know,' I say, beginning to get annoyed. I stop and think for a second before speaking again. In my head I can still see the expression on the man's face. 'He looked absolutely fucking terrified,' I tell them. 'He looked like he was the one who was being attacked.'

2

There's a girl who sits on the other side of the office called Jennifer Reynolds. I don't know her very well. I don't have much to do with her from day to day. In fact I've only spoken to her a handful of times since I was transferred into the PFP. She's not here today and I hate it when she's out. When Jennifer Reynolds isn't here her duties get shared out between the rest of us, and the job I have to cover today is the worst job of all – Reception. The postal address of the PFP isn't actively broadcast but it's on some of the correspondence we send out and it's in the phone book and it doesn't take much for the general public to find out where we are. We get a lot of visitors, too many in my opinion. If someone comes here it's almost always because they've been fined or clamped. They've probably already tried to get the fine overturned or the clamp removed and by the time they reach us coming to argue their case in person is often the only option they have left. So those people who do turn up here are likely to already be seriously pissed off. Shouting, screaming and threatening behaviour isn't unusual. The first place these people reach is Reception, and the first person they get to scream at, shout at or threaten is the poor sod sat behind the desk.

So here I am, sitting alone at the Reception desk, staring at the tatty bronzed-glass entrance door, watching anxiously for any visitors. I hate this. It's like sitting in a dentist's waiting room. I'm constantly watching the clock on the wall. It's hung just above a large notice board covered with unread and unhelpful council posters and notices. Just to the left of the notice board, equally unread and unhelpful, is a small sign which warns the public against intimidating or attacking council staff. The fact that it's there doesn't make me feel any safer. There's a personal attack alarm stuck under the desk but that doesn't make me feel any better either.

It's four thirty-eight. Twenty-two minutes to go then I'm finished for the day.

I'm sure Tina enjoys making me come out here. It's always me who ends up covering for Jennifer. Being out on Reception is a form of torture. You're not allowed to bring any paperwork out here with you (something about protecting confidential data) and the lack of any distractions makes the time drag painfully slowly. So far this afternoon I've only had to deal with two phone calls, and they were just personal calls for members of staff.

Four thirty-nine.

Come on clock, speed up.

Four fifty-four.

Almost there. I'm watching the clock all the time now, willing the hands to move round quickly so that I can get out of here. I'm already rehearsing my escape from the office in my head. I just have to shut down my computer and grab my coat from the cloakroom then I'll sprint to the station. If I can get away quickly enough I might manage to catch the early train and that'll get me back home for . . .

Damn. Bloody phone's ringing again. I hate the way it rings. It grates like an off-key alarm clock and the noise goes right through me. I pick it up and cringe at the thought of what might be waiting for me at the other end of the line.

'Good afternoon, PFP, Danny McCoyne speaking,' I mumble quickly. I've learnt to answer the phone quietly and at speed. It makes it difficult for the caller to take your name.

'Can I speak to Mr Fitzpatrick in Payroll please?' a heavily accented female voice asks. Thank God for that – this isn't a screaming member of the public with a complaint, it's just a wrong number. I relax. We get a few calls for Payroll most days. Their extensions are similar to ours. You'd think someone would do something about it. Anyway I'm relieved. The last thing I want is a problem at four fifty-five.

'You've come through to the wrong department,' I explain. 'You've dialled 2300 instead of 3200. I'll try and transfer you. If you get cut off just dial 1000 and that'll take you through to the main exchange . . .'

I'm suddenly distracted and my voice trails away as the front door flies open. I instinctively move back on my chair, trying to put as much distance as possible between me and whoever it is who's about to come storming into the building. I finish the phone call and allow myself to relax slightly when I see the front wheels of a child's pushchair being forced through the door. The pushchair is jammed in the doorway and I get up to help. A short, rain-soaked woman in a green and purple anorak enters Reception. As well as the child in the pushchair (which is hidden from view by a heavy plastic rain-cover) two more small children follow her inside. The bedraggled family stand in the middle of the Reception area and drip water onto the grubby marble-effect floor. The woman seems harassed and is preoccupied with her kids. She snaps at the tallest child, telling him that 'Mummy has a problem to sort out with this man, then we'll get you back home for something to eat.'

She takes off her hood and I can see that she's in her late thirties or early forties. She's plain-looking and her large, round, rain-splashed glasses are steaming up. Her face is flushed red and there are dribbles of rainwater dripping off the end of her nose. She doesn't make eye contact with me. She slams her handbag down on the desk and begins searching through it. She stops for a moment to lift the rain-cover (which is also beginning to steam up with condensation) and checks on her baby who seems to be sleeping. She returns her attention to the contents of her handbag and I make my way back around to the other side of the counter.

'Can I help you?' I ask cautiously, deciding that it's about time I offered. She glares at me over the rim of her glasses. This woman has an attitude, I can sense it. She's making me feel uncomfortable. I know I'm in for a hard time.

'Wait a minute,' she snaps, talking to me as if I'm one of her kids. She takes a packet of tissues out of her bag and passes one to one of the children at her feet who keeps wiping his nose on his sleeve. 'Blow,' she orders sternly, shoving the tissue into the middle of the kid's face. The child doesn't argue.

I glance up at the clock. Four fifty-seven. Doesn't look like I'll be getting the early train home tonight.

'I parked my car at Leftbank Place for five minutes while I took my eldest son to the toilet,' she begins as she repacks her bag. No time for niceties, she's straight into her complaint. 'In those five minutes my car was clamped. Now I know that I shouldn't have been parked there, but it was only for five minutes and I was only there because it was absolutely necessary. I want to speak to someone who has the authority to sort this out and I want to speak to them now. I want that clamp removed from my car so I can get my children home.'

I clear my throat and get ready to try and respond. Suddenly my mouth is dry and my tongue feels twice its normal size. It had to be Leftbank Place, didn't it. It's an area of waste ground just ten minutes walk from our office. Sometimes it feels like just about every other car that's clamped in this town is clamped at Leftbank Place. The enforcement team who cover that area are notorious. Someone told me they're on some kind of performance-related pay scheme – the more cars they clamp each week, the more they get paid. I don't know whether or not that's true but it doesn't help me now. I know I have no choice but to give this woman a stock response from procedures. I also know that she's not going to like it.

'Madam,' I begin, tensing up in anticipation of her reaction, 'Leftbank Place is a strictly no parking area. The council . . .'

She doesn't give me chance to get any further.

'I'll tell you about the council,' she yells, her voice suddenly uncomfortably loud. 'This bloody council needs to spend less time clamping people and more time making sure that public amenities are in proper working order. The only reason I had to park at bloody Leftbank Place was because the public toilets in Millennium Square have been vandalised! My son has a bowel condition. I didn't have any choice. He couldn't wait any longer.'

'There must have been other toilets . . .' I begin to say, instantly regretting having opened my mouth. Christ I hate this job. I wish I was back dealing with rubbish collections, rat infestations or even broken street lamps again. My biggest problem is that it sounds like this woman has been genuinely hard done by and I'd probably have done exactly the same as she did if I'd been out with my kids. It sounds like she's got a fair point and there's nothing I'd like to do more than call off the clampers but I don't have the authority. My options now are bleak; follow procedures and get yelled at again by this lady or get yelled at by Tina Murray if I don't do things by the book. Chances are I'm going to cop it from both of them. Before she can react to my stupid comment I try and cover it up. 'I understand what you're saying, madam, but . . .'

'Do you?' she screams, this time loud enough to wake the baby in the pushchair who starts to whimper and moan. 'Do you really? I don't think you do, because if you did understand you'd be on the phone to someone right now getting that bloody clamp removed from my car so that I can get my children home. They're cold, they're hungry and . . .'

'I need to just . . .'

'I don't want excuses, I want this dealt with.'

She's not going to listen. This is pointless. She isn't even going to give me a chance.

'Madam . . .'

'I suggest you go and speak to your superiors and find someone who's prepared to take responsibility for this shoddy mess and come and sort it out. I was forced to park at Leftbank Place because of this council's inefficiencies. I have a son who has a medical condition and I needed to get him to the toilet urgently. If the council had done their job properly in the first place and had made sure the public toilets were in full working order then I wouldn't have been parked there, I wouldn't have been clamped and I wouldn't be stood here now talking to someone who clearly can't or won't do anything to help me. I need to speak to someone who's a little higher up the chain of command than the receptionist so why don't you do us both a favour and go and find someone who is actually prepared to do something before my son needs to use the toilet again.'

Patronising bitch. I stand and stare at her, feeling myself getting angrier and angrier. But there's nothing I can do . . .

'Well?' she snaps.

'Just give me a minute, madam,' I stammer. I turn and storm back into the office and walk straight into Tina coming the other way.

'What are you doing in here, Danny?' she asks, her tone of voice as patronising as the woman outside. 'If you're in here, who's manning Reception?'

She knows full well there's no-one out there. I try and explain but I know it's pointless.

'I've got a lady out in Reception who—'

'You should have telephoned through if you needed help,' she interrupts. 'You know the rules, you've been here long enough now. There should always be someone at the Reception desk and you should always telephone through if you have a problem.'

'There is someone at the Reception desk,' I sigh, 'and she's having a real go at me so can I tell you what her problem is please?'

She looks up at the clock. Damn, it's gone five. I'll probably be stuck at the station until six now.

'Make it quick,' she sneers, making it sound as if she's doing me a favour.

'This lady has been clamped because she parked at Leftbank Place—'

'Tough! You can't park at Leftbank Place. There are bloody big signs up everywhere telling you not to park at Leftbank Place.'

This isn't getting any easier.

'I know that, you know that and she knows that. That's not the issue.'

'What do you mean, that's not the issue?'

I pause before speaking again. I know I'm going to have a battle convincing Tina that this lady has a genuine case. For a moment I consider giving up and taking my chances outside in Reception again.

'This lady tells me she parked at Leftbank Place because she needed to take her son to the toilet.'

'What kind of an excuse is that?'

'She needed to take him to the toilet because he has a medical condition and because the public toilets in Millennium Square have been vandalised.'

'That's not our problem—'

'No, but her argument is that it *is* the council's problem. She's demanding we get the clamp removed. Won't go anywhere until it's done.'

'She can't go anywhere,' Tina laughs to herself. 'We'll get the clamp removed when she pays the fine.'

I'm not surprised by her response, just disappointed. I want to go home. I don't want to go out there and get yelled at again. What annoys me most of all it that we both know the longer this lady stands her ground and makes a noise in Reception, the more chance there is that the clamp will be removed. I can't stand all this bullshit and pretence. I can't help but say something.

'Come on, Tina, give me a break. You know as well as I do that if she shouts long enough we'll let her off.'

She looks at me, chews her gum and shrugs her shoulders.

'That's as maybe, but we have to try and take the fee from the client first. You know the procedure. We have to—'

There's no point listening to any more of this rubbish. I can't be bothered.

'I know the bloody procedure,' I sigh as I turn my back on her and trudge back towards Reception. I wonder whether I should just keep going? Should I walk straight past the woman and her kids and just leave the building and the job behind?

I open the door and she turns round to glare at me. The expression on her face is pure evil.

'Well?'

I take a deep breath.

'I've had a word with my supervisor,' I begin dejectedly, knowing what's coming next. 'We can get the clamp removed, but we must insist on payment of the charge indicated on the signs displayed at Leftbank Place. We can't—'

And she's off. She explodes again, shouting and yelling at me. The force, velocity and ferocity of her outburst is remarkable. It's an incredible (but not at all unexpected) rant and I have no defence. I can't argue because I happen to think she has a valid case. If she'd just shut up for a second I might be able to . . . oh, what's the use? I don't know why I bother. The more she shouts at me the less I'm inclined to listen. I've given up trying to follow what she's saying now. Her words have just become a constant stream of noise. I'll wait for her to take a breath.

'Madam,' I interrupt quickly as she pauses to inhale. I hold my hand up in front of me to make it clear that it's my turn to speak. 'I'll go and get my supervisor.'

I walk away, ignoring the muttered comments I can hear about 'speaking to the organ grinder, not the monkey'. I'm long past caring. As I reach for the office door Tina pulls it open from the other side and barges past me. She stops just long enough to hiss a few venomous words in my direction.

'Well handled,' she sneers sarcastically. 'You're bloody useless, you are. I could hear her shouting from my desk. Now what's her name?'

'Don't know,' I admit, cringing at the fact that I haven't even managed to establish the most basic of details.

'Bloody useless,' she sneers again before fixing a false smile on her foul face and marching over to the bedraggled woman and her children. 'My name's Tina Murray,' she says, 'how can I help you?'

I lean against the office door and watch the predictable charade being played out. Tina listens to the complaint, points out to the lady that she really shouldn't have been parked at Leftbank Place, then makes a phone call to 'see what she can do'. Ten minutes later and the clamp is removed. Tina looks fantastic and I look like an idiot. I knew it would happen like that.

Five thirty-two.

I run to the station and reach the platform just in time to see the next train leave.

3

The one slight advantage of leaving the office late tonight was that, for once, I was able to get a seat on the train home. It's usually packed and I'm left standing in-between carriages, surrounded by other equally pissed-off travellers. I needed the space to help me relax and calm down tonight. While I was waiting on the platform I decided I should spend the journey home trying to work out what it is I actually want to do with my life and how I'm going to go about making it happen. I have similar useless discussions with myself on the way home at least once or twice every week. I was too tired to concentrate tonight. There were two girls sitting opposite me and their conversation about clothes, soap operas and who'd done what with whose boyfriend was far more interesting than anything I was thinking about.

February. I hate this time of year. It's cold, wet and depressing. It's dark when I leave the house in the morning and it's dark when I get home at night. This time tomorrow, I keep reminding myself, it will be the weekend. Two days without work. I can't wait.

I drag myself up the hill and around the corner into Calder Grove and I can finally see our home at the end of the road. It's not much but it's all we've got at the moment and it will have to do for now. We're on the council waiting list to get a bigger place but it'll probably be years before they move us. Now that Lizzie is working again we might finally be able to start saving so that we can put a deposit on a house of our own and get out of this apartment block. We'd planned to move a couple of years ago but she fell pregnant with Josh and everything got put on hold again. I love my kids but we didn't plan any of them. We were just starting to get back on our feet after having Edward and Ellis but then Josh came along and we found it hard to put food on the table, never mind money in the bank. We claim all the benefits we're entitled to and Harry, Lizzie's dad, helps us out now and again, but it's a constant struggle. It shouldn't have to be like this. Still, we get more help from Liz's dad than we do from my family. Mum's in Spain with her new boyfriend, my brother's in Australia and no-one's heard anything from Dad for three years now. The only time we hear from any of them is on the children's birthdays and at Christmas.

There's a gang of kids under a broken street lamp in the alleyway which runs between two of the houses on my right. I see them there most nights, smoking and drinking and driving beat-up cars around the estate. I don't like them. They're trouble. I put my head down and walk a little faster. I worry about my children growing up round here. Calder Grove itself isn't that bad but some parts of this estate are rough and things are getting worse. The council is trying to run apartment blocks like ours down so they can flatten them and build new houses. There are six flats in our block – two on each floor – and only ours and one other is left occupied now. We try not to have anything to do with the people upstairs. I don't trust them. Gary and Chris, I think they're called. Two middle-aged men who live together on the top floor. They don't seem short of cash but neither of them ever seem to go out to work either. And there's a constant stream of visitors ringing their doorbell at all hours of the day and night. I'm sure they're selling something up there, but I don't think I want to know what it is.

I finally reach the communal front door and let myself into the apartment block. The door sticks and then opens with a loud, ear-piercing creak which can probably be heard from halfway down the street. I've been trying to get the council to come and sort it out for months but they don't want to know, even though I work for them. Inside the building the entrance hall is dark and cold and my footsteps echo all around me. The kids hate this lobby and I understand why. They get scared out here. I wouldn't want to spend too long out here on my own either. I unlock the flat, go inside and shut, lock and bolt the door behind me. Home. Thank God for that. I take off my coat and shoes and, for almost half a second, I relax.

'Where've you been?' Lizzie scowls. She appears from Edward and Josh's room and crosses the hallway diagonally to the kitchen. Her arms are piled high with dirty washing.

'Work,' I reply. The answer's so obvious I wonder whether it's a trick question. 'Why?'

'You should have been back ages ago.'

'Sorry, I got delayed. Got stuck with some woman having a go at me. I missed my train.'

'You could have called.'

'I've run out of credit on my mobile and I didn't have any cash on me to top it up. Sorry, Liz, I didn't think I'd be this late.'

No response. I can't even see her now. The fact she's gone quiet on me is ominous. Something's wrong and I know that whatever it is, any problems that I might have had today will now have to take second place. All my worries will pale into insignificance alongside whatever it is that's bothering her. This seems to happen almost every day and it's really beginning to piss me off. I know Lizzie works hard and the kids play her up, but she wants to think herself lucky. She wants to try dealing with some of the shit that I have to put up with each day. I take a deep breath and follow her into the kitchen.

'Your dinner's in the oven,' she grunts.

'Thanks,' I mumble as I open the oven door and recoil from the sudden blast of red-hot air which comes from it. I pick up a tea towel and use it to grip the edge of a dried-out and overcooked plate of pie, chips and peas. 'Are you okay?'

'Not really,' she replies, her voice barely audible. She's on her knees shoving washing into the machine.

'What's the matter?'

'Nothing.'

I crunch into a burnt chip and then quickly smother the rest of my food in sauce to take away some of the charcoal taste. Don't want to risk Lizzie thinking I don't like it. I hate playing these games. It's obvious something's wrong, so why won't she just tell me what it is? Why do we have to go through this stupid routine every time she has something on her mind? I decide to try again.

'I can tell something's wrong.'

'Very perceptive of you,' she mumbles. 'It doesn't matter.'

'Obviously it does.'

'Look,' she sighs, switching on the washing machine and standing up and stretching her back, 'if you really want to know what's wrong why don't you ask the kids? Maybe they'll tell you why I . . .'

Right on cue two of the children push their way into the kitchen, jostling with each other for position. Edward digs his elbow into his little sister's ribs. Ellis shoves him back out of the way and then slams against the table, spilling Liz's coffee.

'Dad, will you tell her?' Ed spits, pointing accusingly.

'Tell her what?' I ask, distracted by the pile of bills I've just found on the table.

'Tell her to stop following me around,' he yells. 'She's winding me up.'

'Why don't you both just leave each other alone? Go and play in your own rooms.'

'I want to watch telly,' Ed protests.

'I was watching it first,' Ellis complains.

'She'll be going to bed soon,' I sigh, trying to reason with Edward. 'Just let her watch it for a while then you can change the channel when she's gone to bed.'

'But my programme's on now,' he whines, not having any of it. 'It's not fair, you always take her side. Why do you always take her side?'

I've had enough.

'Let's just leave the television off then,' I tell them. Both of them start screaming at me but even their God-awful noise is drowned out by Lizzie who shrieks at the pair of them to get out of her sight at a deafening volume. Ed pushes his sister as he barges out of the room. Ellis slaps him on the back as he passes.

'Well handled,' Liz mumbles sarcastically.

'Little sods,' I mumble back.

'That's why I've had enough,' she snaps. 'I've had to put up with their rubbish constantly since we came out of school and I can't stand it any more. Okay?'

She storms out of the room. I don't bother following, there's no point. There's nothing I can do or say to make things any easier so I take the easy option and do and say nothing.

FRIDAY

ii

'**H**e was looking at me.'

'Get lost! He was looking at me. He's not interested in you!'

Josie Stone and her best friend Shona Robertson walked down Sparrow Hill and across the park together arm in arm, laughing as they discussed Darren Francis, a boy two years ahead of them at school who they'd just passed outside Shona's house.

'Anyway,' Josie teased, 'everyone knows that Kevin Braithwaite fancies you. You stick with Kevin and leave me and Darren alone.'

'Kevin Braithwaite?!' Shona protested. 'I wouldn't be seen dead with him. He's more your type.'

'Shut up!'

The two friends tripped and slid down the greasy grassy bank, still giggling and holding onto each other's arms as they struggled to keep their footing. Their speed increased as they stumbled further down the hill and onto level ground. Josie slipped as they ran across the middle of a muddy football pitch. Shona instinctively reached out and yanked her back up before she hit the ground.

'Careful!' she laughed as she struggled to stay standing like a bad ice skater.

Josie and Shona were as close as sisters. They'd met at school three years ago and, both being only children, had quickly become inseparable. They spent almost all of their free time together and often slept over at each other's house. Last summer Josie had even spent a fortnight in Spain with Shona and her family. Nothing was allowed to come between them, not even boys.

'I heard that Dayne was round Phillipa's house last night,' Shona said, suddenly remembering a vital piece of gossip she'd heard on the way home from school. 'She's a dirty tramp that Phillipa.'

Josie stopped walking.

Shona carried on for a few seconds, oblivious.

'Danni said she saw her with her hands down . . .'

27

When she realised she was on her own she stopped, turned round and looked at her friend.

'What's the matter with you?' she asked. Josie didn't answer. 'Come on you silly cow, the others will have gone if we don't get a move on.'

Still Josie didn't move. She simply stood and stared at Shona who, not understanding her friend's behaviour, turned round again and continued walking towards the shops and the group of girls from school they'd arranged to meet there.

Josie broke into a sudden sprint. She ran directly at Shona and shoved her in the back between her shoulder blades, knocking her off her feet and down into the long wet grass. She tried to stand but before she could get up Josie kicked her in the stomach. She rolled her over onto her back and whined in pain.

'What the hell are you doing, you silly bitch?'

Josie didn't answer. Instead she simply dropped her knees onto Shona's exposed chest, forcing every scrap of air from her lungs. Shona gagged with surprise and shock as she struggled to breathe in. Stunned and wide-eyed she stared into Josie's face.

'Why did you . . . ?' she began to say. Josie wasn't listening. She'd found a stone half-buried in the mud and grass nearby and was desperately digging her fingers around its edge, trying to pull it out of the ground. Panting with effort she picked up the heavy, brick-sized rock and held it high above her head.

'Josie, don't . . .' Shona whimpered.

Holding it with both hands, Josie brought the stone crashing down on her friend's chest. She felt her ribs crack and splinter under the force of the undefended impact. In too much sudden pain to scream, Shona groaned in agony and watched helplessly as Josie lifted the stone again and brought it down on her for a second time. She hit her with such savage force that a broken rib punctured one of her lungs. Her breathing became erratic and rasping, then desperately shallow and forced. Her shattered ribcage began to move with sudden, juddering movements as her damaged body struggled to continue to function.

Josie leant down over her dying friend and looked deep into her face. Her skin was ghostly white, smeared with splashes of mud and dribbles of blood which now gurgled and bubbled from the corners of her mouth. Her dark, panic-filled eyes began to glaze *over and lose their focus. She was aware of Josie lifting the stone again, but nothing more.*

She knew that her friend was dead but Josie had to be certain. She smashed the rock into her face, breaking her left cheekbone and almost dislocating her jaw. Exhausted with effort she rolled away from the corpse and sat panting on the wet grass nearby.

Josie stared at the sprawling dark shadows of the town below her. She couldn't go down there now. She couldn't go home either. She didn't know where she was going to go or what she was going to do. Maybe she could just stay in the park and hope no-one comes looking, she thought. Either that or she'd have to take her chances and just run.

She hadn't had any choice. She'd had to kill Shona. She felt no guilt or remorse for what she'd done, just relief.

4

We're out. We've escaped. For the first time in months Lizzie and I have managed to get away from the house together without any of the children in tow. I can't remember the last time we were out together like this. The fact that we're crammed into a small, dark and sweaty concert hall with six or seven hundred other people doesn't seem to matter. The gig hasn't even started yet but the background music is already deafening and the lighting is virtually non-existent. The chances of us actually managing to speak to each other are slim.

'Doesn't feel right, does it?' Liz shouts at me. She has to lift herself up onto tiptoes to yell into my ear.

'What doesn't?' I shout back.

'Not having the kids here. I'm not used to it. I keep looking round expecting to see at least one of them.'

'Make the most of it,' I tell her. 'How long's it been since we went out together on our own?'

'Months,' she screams, struggling to make herself heard over the noise.

The conversation is over quickly. The effort of having to yell at each other is already making my throat sore and the gig hasn't even started yet. I watch the stage as roadies and other crew members check the lights, the sound and the instruments. How long does it take them to get ready? They seem to have been setting things up for ages, there can't be long left to wait now. Someone's going round putting towels and drinks down and gaffer-taping set lists to the floor.

Christ, what was that? Something hit me from the side and I'm down on the floor before I know what's happened. I try to stand up quickly, my heart thumping in my chest. Liz grabs my arm and pulls me to my feet. I don't want any trouble tonight. I'm not good at dealing with confrontation. I really don't want any trouble.

'Sorry, mate,' an over-excited and half-drunk fan shouts at me.

He's holding two (now) half-empty drinks in his hands and I can tell from his blurred and directionless eyes that he's off his face on drugs or booze or both. We're standing close to the mixing desk and there's a carpet-covered bump running along the floor next to us which protects the power cables I think. Looks like this idiot has tripped up the step and gone flying. He mumbles something about being sorry again and then staggers off deeper into the crowd.

'You all right?' Liz asks, wiping splashes of drink from my shirt.

'Fine,' I answer quickly. My heart's still beating at ten times its normal speed. Relieved, I pull Lizzie towards me and wrap my arms around her. Having her next to me makes me feel safe. It's not often we're able to be this close any more. That's the price you pay for having too many kids too quickly in a flat that's too small. Funny how we can stand in a room with the best part of a thousand strangers and have less chance of being interrupted than at home with just three children.

Lizzie turns round and lifts herself up onto tiptoes to speak to me again.

'Think Dad's okay?' she asks.

'Why shouldn't he be?' I yell back.

'I worry that he thinks we're taking advantage of him. He's already there looking after Josh most days now and he's there again tonight with all three of them. It's a lot to ask. He's not getting any younger and I think he's starting to get fed up with it.'

'I know he is. He had a go at me before we left.'

'What did he say?'

How much do I tell her? Harry and I don't get on but we try and stay civil for Lizzie's sake. He was not at all happy tonight but I know he wouldn't want Lizzie to worry about it.

'Nothing much,' I answer, shrugging my shoulders, 'he just grumbled something about him seeing more of the kids than I do. He made some bad joke about Josh calling him Daddy instead of me.'

'He's trying to wind you up. Just ignore him.'

'He's always trying to wind me up.'

'It's just his age.'

'That's a crap excuse.'

'Just ignore him,' she says again.

'It doesn't bother me,' I shout, lying and trying to save her

32

feelings. The truth is Harry is seriously beginning to piss me off and it's getting to the point where I can see us coming to blows.

'So what did you say to him?'

'I just told him how we appreciate what he does for us and reminded him that it's been at least four months since you and I last went out together on our own.'

'He's just trying to get you to react . . .' she starts to say. She stops speaking and turns around quickly when the lights suddenly fade. The crowd erupts into life as the members of the band walk through the shadows and step out onto the stage. After a few seconds delay the music starts and I forget about Harry and everything else.

This is the fourth time I've seen The Men They Couldn't Hang. It's been a couple of years since I last saw them and it's great to see them again. I've been looking forward to tonight since I booked the tickets a couple of months ago. I never get enough of the adrenaline rush of hearing good music played live and played loud like this. Hearing these songs again snatches me out of the day to day and helps me forget all the things I usually waste my time worrying about. I hold Lizzie close. As long as the music's playing I don't have to do anything except listen, relax and enjoy myself.

Six or seven songs in now – not sure exactly how many – and this place is really alive. The hall is packed and there's a brilliant atmosphere here. Swill plays the opening notes to one of my favourite tracks and I recognise it instantly, way ahead of most of the crowd. I feel the hairs on the back of my neck stand on end and I squeeze Lizzie tighter. She knows just how much I love this.

They've really hit their stride now and it's like they've never been away. Hearing this music again brings back so many memories. I remember the first time I heard this song on the radio just after I passed my driving test. I'd just bought my first car. It was an old heap that cost more to insure than it did to buy and me and a few mates had gone down to . . .

Swill has stopped playing.

Strange. He was strumming his guitar and singing but he's just stopped. The rest of the band have carried on without him. It's like he's forgotten where he is and what he's supposed to be doing. He's let go of his guitar and it's hanging by the strap around his neck now, swinging from side to side. This guy has just spent the last forty minutes playing and singing his heart out but now he's just standing completely still centre stage, head bowed and staring at the microphone in front of him. Has he forgotten the words? Bloody hell, he's been doing this for long enough. Surely it can't be stage fright or anything like that? Is there a technical problem? Maybe he's ill? The rest of the music continues for a few bars longer. One by one the rest of the band realise that something's wrong. The lead guitarist has stopped now, and he's staring at Swill trying to work out what the hell's going on. McGuire, the bass player, comes to a faltering stop just leaving the drummer to pound out a few more empty and unaccompanied beats before he stops too. Now Lizzie, me, the rest of the band and the entire audience are staring at the slowly swaying figure of Swill standing awkwardly in the spotlight.

The crowd doesn't like it. For a few seconds there's been an uneasy quiet but now the audience is beginning to turn. People are shouting out insults and there's a slow handclap starting. I've got no idea what's wrong. It makes me feel nervous. Just wish something would happen . . .

I think he's about to walk off. Swill takes a couple of steps back and then stops. Now he's taken hold of his guitar and he's swung it round his head so that it's no longer hanging round his neck. He's standing still again now, looking around the stage, oblivious to the jeers and shouts from the hundreds of people who are staring at him and yelling at him to get on with it and start playing. Cush starts to approach him and now Swill moves. He suddenly bursts into life and moves quickly and unexpectedly to his left. Holding the guitar by its neck he swings it around again, now gripping it like a weapon. He lunges towards Simmonds, the lead guitarist, and swings the instrument round once more, catching him full on the side of his head. Simmonds tried to lift his hand to block the blow but the attack was so quick and unexpected that he wasn't able to properly defend himself. The force of the impact has sent him reeling back into the drum kit, clutching his jaw. But that's not the end of it. Swill is standing over him now and he's started smashing the guitar down on him again and again. Bloody hell, he's hitting him so hard that the wooden instrument has begun to splinter and smash. I don't understand. Maybe they had an argument before they came on stage or something like that? This guy has always made a big deal out of the fact that he's a pacifist. Now look at him! What the hell did Simmonds do to deserve this? McGuire is trying to separate them now . . .

The audience is starting to turn nasty. We've stood together and watched in disbelief but now people are starting to react to what they're seeing. Many of the people right down at the front are trying to push their way out, a small minority are cheering on the violence and are trying to get closer chanting, 'Swill, Swill . . .' and egging him on. Most of us are just stood staring at the stage. I look up again and I can hardly believe what I'm seeing. Swill is standing centre stage again now, swinging a metal microphone stand around in a wide arc. Simmonds is flat on his back in what's left of the drum kit and he's not moving. McGuire's crawling across the stage on his hands and knees, trying to get to him. Now two roadies have rushed Swill. One of them catches the full force of a swipe with the mike stand right across his chest, the other dives and wraps himself around the musician's waist and tries to grapple him down. He's having none of it. He kicks and punches him off and tries to scramble away. He trips over the monitors and disappears down into the dark pit between the stage and the security barriers. There's a wail of feedback that sounds like a scream.

Lost him.

Can't see him.

Suddenly he appears again. He's pushed his way out through the barriers and is running into the crowd. His MAG T-shirt is ripped and now hangs round his neck like a rag. The audience react with a strange mixture of fear and adulation. Some people run away from him, others run towards him.

'Let's go,' Lizzie shouts to me.

'What?'

'I want to go,' she says again. 'Now, Danny, please. I want to go.'

People are starting to try and move away from the stage area in large numbers. The house lights come up and everyone's speed suddenly seems to increase now that they can see where they're going. We're pushed and jostled towards the exits by shocked and frightened people criss-crossing in every direction, trying to get away from the trouble before it gets any worse. In the middle of the hall the fighting starts to look like a fully fledged riot. I can't see what's happened to Swill but scores of fans who are either pissed or stoned or who just enjoy a good fight have dived into the middle of the chaos with their fists flying.

There's already a bottleneck forming where the bulk of the crowd is struggling to get out of the venue. I grab Lizzie's hand and pull her towards the nearest exit. We're surrounded by people and our speed reduces to a painfully slow shuffle. A mass of huge, shaven-headed security guards push their way into the hall through another door to our left. I'm not sure whether they're here to try and stop the fighting or just to join in. I don't want to wait around to find out.

Through the double doors, down a short, steep, stone staircase and we finally push our way out onto the street. It's pouring with rain and there are people everywhere running in all directions.

I have no idea what just happened in there.

'You okay?' I ask Lizzie. She nods. She looks shocked and scared.

'I'm all right,' she answers. 'I just want to go home.'

I grab her hand tighter still and pull her through the bemused crowds. Some people are hanging around the front of the venue but most seem to be leaving. I'm really fucking angry but I'm trying not to show it. That's just typical of how things seem to be working out for me at the moment. Why does everything have to be so difficult? I just wanted to relax and switch off and enjoy myself for once, but what happens? A long-time musical hero loses all his credibility and fucks up my first night out with Liz in months. Fucking typical. Bloody prima donna.

We slip down a side street and run back to the car.

SATURDAY

5

Half past six and the alarm clock wakes me up with its usual grating groan. I reach out and fumble around in the darkness to switch it off. I have to think for a minute to try and remember what day it is. Do I have to get up? I'm sure it's Saturday and I just forgot to cancel the alarm. I lie still for a second and try and work back through yesterday and last night. I can remember another dull day at the office with Tina Murray taking me into one of the interview rooms and ripping into me because of my attitude. I remember the gig and the fight and running away from the venue. Christ, what exactly did happen there last night? Doesn't matter now. All that's important is that it's Saturday and I don't have to get up and go to work.

I roll over onto my side and put my arm around Lizzie. She seemed happier yesterday than she has been for a while. It did us both good to get out and spend some time together. Shame it had to end the way it did. When we got back to the flat I had to drive Harry home. After that we opened a couple of cans of beer and sat in front of the TV watching a dumb action film, numbing our brains.

I shuffle a little closer to Liz and then wait for her to react. When she doesn't respond I move a little closer again and press myself up tight against her. We never seem to have chance to be intimate these days. Long gone are the times when we could be free and jump into bed at the drop of a hat. These days there's always something to do or someone to look after first. Having kids has changed everything. I wish I'd been allowed to borrow someone else's for a while before we had our own. I never appreciated just how much having children can screw up your previously simple and uncomplicated life.

I can feel Lizzie's skin through the cloth of her pyjamas. She feels beautifully soft and warm. If it wasn't so early I might take a chance and try and slip my hand inside her top. Sometimes, if I'm careful and gentle enough, a move like that might start something. At this time of the day, though, she's more likely to kick me than caress me. But I can remember a time a couple of weeks back when we were both in the kitchen. She'd brushed up against me while I was standing at the sink doing the washing-up. I stopped and turned around and she just looked at me like she does sometimes. I kissed her and I couldn't help myself. I grabbed her with wet hands and pushed her back onto the table. She took off her top and . . .

'I want my breakfast, Daddy,' Ellis pipes up from somewhere in the darkness at the side of the bed. Christ, she scared me half to death. I had no idea she was there. My suddenly semi-formed erection quickly droops back down to nothing.

'It's too early,' I mumble. 'Go back to bed.'

'I'm hungry, Daddy,' she says, undeterred.

'In a bit.'

'I'm hungry now. I can't wait.'

'Later.'

'Now,' she demands with more force and insistence in her voice than I would ever have expected from a four-and-a-half-year-old. She's not going anywhere. I'll have to try a different tack.

'Why don't you get into bed with Mummy and me for a while, sweetheart,' I suggest hopefully, quickly giving up all thoughts of sex. 'We'll get up and get your breakfast in a few minutes.' An hour or so with Ellis in the bed seems a much better option than getting up now. I expect a little resistance but, to my surprise, she agrees. She drags herself up onto the bed, steps over my head and then wriggles between Lizzie and I. Christ, her feet are cold. Lizzie angrily mumbles something unintelligible when they touch her.

Thirty seconds of silence and she starts on me again.

'I want toast please, Daddy,' she says. I have to give her her due, she might be irritating but at least she's polite.

'In a minute,' I yawn, rolling over onto my side again, grabbing back some duvet and twisting and contorting my body to avoid contact with her icy feet. 'Let's just stay in bed for a little longer, shall we . . . ?'

She agrees but she talks. And she talks. And she keeps talking. I screw my eyes shut and pull the duvet over my head.

*

I managed to last another twenty minutes with Ellis in bed before admitting defeat and getting up. I'm in the kitchen now waiting for the kettle to boil. We're both dressed and Ellis has had her breakfast but she's still talking non-stop about nothing in particular. Lizzie's still in bed. She could sleep through anything. Wish I could.

It's freezing cold in here. This flat is impossible to heat. I think it's so cold because the rest of the building is virtually empty. We're on the left-hand side of the ground floor and all the warmth that our old-fashioned heating system generates just rises up and disappears into the empty flats above us. I've even thought about trying to get us moved upstairs to see if that makes any difference.

I grab my drink and a bowl of cereal and sit down in front of the TV. There's nothing on worth watching; crappy cartoons, cookery and lifestyle programmes and loud, intelligence-insulting kids shows are all I can find. I settle on the news but even the headlines are boring this morning (an outbreak of violence in the capital, a sex scandal involving a politician and his nephew, more warnings about climate change and a celebrity death). I'll wait for the sports headlines. They're usually on just before the hour.

Christ, all the kids are out of bed now. Why do they have to get up so early? We have to drag them out of their beds when it's a school day. They've only been up for a couple of minutes and I can already hear Ed and Josh fighting over something. I close my eyes and wait for them to start on me. It's only a matter of time . . .

'I want to watch Channel 22,' Ed says as he storms into the room. Does his entire life revolve around TV?

'I'm watching this,' I answer quickly, annoyed that I've been disturbed.

'With your eyes shut?' he sneers in an irritating tone which makes me want to slap him.

'Yes, with my eyes shut,' I sneer back. 'I'm waiting to watch something.'

'I really need to watch Channel 22, Dad,' he whines.

'Watch it in your room,' I suggest sensibly. We bought Ed a TV last Christmas. He hardly uses the damn thing.

'I can't get Channel 22 in there.'

'Sorry, son, I'm watching this. You can turn over when it's finished.'

'That's not fair,' he yells at me, 'I never get to watch any of my programmes.'

Little shit. He seems to spend all of his time in front of the box. How often do I get a turn? It's my TV and I can watch what I like, when I like. I don't know why but I find myself trying to justify watching a five-minute programme to my eight-year-old son.

'You're always watching TV. It's all I ever see you do.'

'No it isn't. It's not fair, you never let me watch what I want.'

I can hear the sports bulletin theme music playing. I open my eyes. Ed's standing directly between me and the TV screen.

'Look, this is only on for five minutes. Let me watch it then you can have your channel on.'

'It's my turn to choose,' Ellis pipes up. I didn't even know she was in here. That's twice she's done that to me today.

'No it isn't,' Ed shouts. 'I'm watching my channel next.'

'But you've got your own telly. I haven't got one. That's not fair, is it, Daddy?'

'It's just tough. I asked first.'

'I asked Mummy last night. She said I could watch what I wanted to this morning. She said that—'

'Will you both just shut up!' I yell, loud enough for the people in the flat on the top floor to hear. I hold my head in my hands in despair. Through the gaps between my fingers I can see the TV screen. The sports reporter is in full flow but I can't hear a damn word she's saying.

'Tell her, Dad,' Ed barks again, not about to let it drop. 'I'm watching my channel next.'

'No you're not. Mummy said that I could—'

'I don't care, Dad said that—'

'Shut up!' I snap. 'For crying out loud, will you both just shut up.'

'She started it,' Ed whines.

'No, he started it,' Ellis whines back, and so it goes on . . .

That's it. The brief sports bulletin is over. Waste of bloody time. Less than five minutes was all I wanted. Was that too much to ask? I get up and switch off the television and for a single blissful moment the flat is completely silent.

'If I can't watch it, no-one can,' I tell them both.

For another second they just stare at me in stunned silence. Then they turn.

'That's not fair,' Ed screams, his face flushed red with anger. 'You can't do that.'

'I just did, now shut up.'

The room is suddenly filled with more noise than ever as they both protest at the same time. It's loud enough to bring Josh waddling in. He starts screaming just because the other two are. I ignore the lot of them. I push past them all and storm through the flat to the bathroom. I sit down on the toilet. The lock on the door is broken and I have to push my foot against it to keep it closed and to keep the kids out.

'Dad, will you tell him,' Ed shouts from just outside the bathroom. Christ, is there no escape? What do I have to do to get some peace and quiet? 'Dad, Josh is messing with the remote control.'

I can't bring myself to answer. I know he knows I'm in here but I just can't bring myself to speak to him. I push my foot a little harder against the door as Ed tries to push his way in from the other side.

'Dad . . . Dad, I know you're in there . . .'

I let my head loll back on my shoulders and I look up at the ceiling. Out of the corner of my eye I can see the window. It's pretty small but we're on the ground floor and I reckon I could squeeze through if I really tried.

Jesus Christ, what am I thinking?

Am I seriously considering trying to escape from my own house through the toilet window? Bloody hell, there has to be more to life than this.

iii

Chris Spencer had been laying the drive in Beechwood Avenue for almost a day and a half and the job was not far off finished. It was a cash-in-hand job on the side for Jackie, a friend of a friend of his girlfriend. He'd started digging out and laying the foundations first thing yesterday morning and now, Saturday lunchtime, he was two-thirds of the way through putting down the block paving. It was hard, physical work and he was on his own today after being let down by his brother who, for a few quid, usually helped him out with jobs like this. It was a cold day but at least it was dry now. It had been raining earlier and he'd started to wonder whether all the effort and the loss of his usual Saturday morning lie-in would be worth the wad of cash he was hoping to shove in his back pocket.

The wheelbarrow was empty again. Tired and hungry he stood up and brushed the sand off his knees, ready to fetch another load of paving bricks. A couple more hours hard graft, he thought, and that would be everything but the edging stones done. He pushed the barrow over towards the half-empty pallet on the grass verge at the side of the road. His calculations had been just about spot-on, he smiled to himself. He'd quoted Jackie for two and a half pallets of bricks but it looked like the job was only going to need two. He'd shove the rest of the bricks in the back of the van and use them on the next job. It wasn't much of a saving but it all helped. It was all profit.

He was halfway through filling the barrow when the motorbike pulled up beside him. It was a huge, powerful thing with a wide exhaust and an impossibly loud engine. He'd heard it approaching from the bottom of the hill. Must be Jackie's son, he thought. She'd said something about him coming over to see her this afternoon. He glanced up and nodded an acknowledgement to the rider as he parked his machine and rested it on the kickstand. The leather-clad figure flicked back his visor and took off his helmet.

'All right, mate, how you getting on?' he asked. 'Mum said it was looking good.'

'Almost done now,' Spencer replied, loading the last few bricks into the barrow and standing up straight. He stretched his back and looked across at the other man. 'Couple of hours and I should be finished. Just got to get the rest of these bricks down and finish off the edges. I think it's . . .'

He stopped speaking and stared into Jackie's son's face.

'What's the matter?'

Spencer couldn't answer. He couldn't speak. He was filled with a sudden, indescribable sense of panic and fear. His heart thumping in his chest, he took a couple of nervous backwards steps towards the house and tripped up the lip of the bricks he'd already laid, landing on his backside. The other man walked towards him and held out his hand to help him up.

'You feeling okay, mate? Want me to get you a drink of water or something?'

Spencer recoiled. He scrambled back to his feet, grabbing a heavy lump hammer as he got up. He launched himself at Jackie's son and wrapped his left hand round his throat. Knocked off balance the two men fell awkwardly to the ground, Jackie's son on his back with Spencer on top, pinning him down.

Spencer lifted the lump hammer and brought over a kilogram of metal smashing down into the middle of the other man's face, caving in his forehead and the bridge of his nose and killing him almost instantly. He lifted the gore-covered hammer and bludgeoned what was left of his face another five times, leaving his head virtually concave, hollowed out like a deflated football.

Spencer got up and stood breathless over the corpse before being thrown off balance again. Jackie, wailing like a banshee, ran from the front of the house and shoved him away from the body of her son. She screamed and dropped to the ground when she saw the hole in his head and the mass of splintered bone and pulped flesh where his face used to be. She looked up at Spencer but all she saw was the bloodied edge of the lump hammer as he swung it towards her.

6

'We're going to be late,' Lizzie grumbles. I know we are, but there's not a lot I can do about it. If she'd given me more notice that we were supposed to be taking Edward to a friend's birthday party then we would have been fine. Half an hour to get the kids ready and out isn't enough. Part of me wishes she'd forgotten about it for another hour. I want Ed to have a good time and enjoy himself, of course I do, but I'm not looking forward to spending the next couple of hours sitting in a kid-friendly and adult-unfriendly 'fun barn' attached to the side of a pub. It's not how I'd planned to spend my Saturday afternoon.

'We'll get there when we get there,' I tell her. 'Getting wound up about it isn't going to help.'

'I'm not wound up,' she snaps, proving that she is. 'I just don't like being late, that's all.'

'We won't be late. We've got a few minutes yet. The pub's only round the corner.'

'I know but look at the traffic.'

'There's probably been an accident or something,' I tell her, sitting up in my seat and craning my neck to try and see further down the road. 'I think there's something going on at the top of the hill. Once we get past that the traffic will clear.'

I hear a muffled thump and a yelp from behind me. I glance over my shoulder and glare at the kids who are crammed shoulder to shoulder on the back seat. They hate being in the car nearly as much as I do. It's too small for us all to fit in but what can I do? I can't afford to change it so they'll just have to put up with it for now. We all will. Lizzie looks at them and then leans closer to me.

'We're going to have to feed them,' she whispers, keeping her voice low so they don't hear.

'Ed will eat at the party, won't he?'

'Yes, but—'

'We'll get the other two a packet of crisps or something,' I say quickly before she gets any ideas. I think I know where this is heading.

'They'll need more than that,' she says. 'We're going to be out for a couple of hours. Why don't we just make it easy for ourselves and have a meal.'

'Because we can't afford it.'

'Come on, Danny, we might as well. We're going to be sat in the pub anyway.'

'We can't afford it,' I say again. How much clearer do I need to make it? 'Look, we'll drop Ed off then go back home and have some dinner. I'll come back and pick him up again after the party.'

'Is it worth all the hassle and the extra petrol? Let's just stop and have a meal and we can—'

'We can't afford it,' I snap for the third time as we reach the top of the hill and pass whatever it is that's been slowing down the traffic. I look into the rear-view mirror and see that the kids are pressing their faces against the glass, trying to see what's going on. 'Don't stare,' I shout at them. I can't help but look myself. Looks like the police have sealed off the entrance to one of the roads which leads off Maple Street.

'Twenty quid,' Lizzie continues. Bloody hell, she's not going to give up. 'Are you telling me you can't find twenty quid to feed your family?'

'Yes,' I answer, trying hard not to get annoyed, 'that's exactly what I'm telling you.' I'm determined she's not going to get the better of me today, no matter how hard she tries. 'I haven't got twenty quid and even if I had, why should I spend it on a meal when we've got a freezer full of food at home? At home we can eat twice as much for half the cost.'

'When was the last time we ate out?'

'When was the last time I had enough money to take us out?'

'Come on, Danny . . .'

I'm not even going to answer. I'll keep my mouth shut and concentrate on driving. She does this to me too often. She's like a dog with a bone. She won't let go. She just keeps nagging and piling on the pressure until I relent just to shut her up.

Not today.

*

48

I caved in. I'm disappointed with myself but it was inevitable. She just wouldn't stop. She kept on and on at me all the way here. I figured I could either relent and take the hit to my wallet or I could stand my ground and risk a whole weekend of grief and her not talking to me. When I walked into the pub and smelled the food and looked at the menu my resistance crumbled. Pathetic really.

We've been waiting for our dinner for almost half an hour now and I'm starting to think they might have forgotten our order. We're tucked out of the way in a corner of the main dining area and the place is heaving. It's Saturday lunchtime so I expected it to be busy but not like this. The long, horseshoe-shaped bar is surrounded by a crowd of bodies several drinkers deep. I should have seen it coming really. There's a football match on this after-noon. It's a local derby between two teams at the bottom of the table and there's a lot at stake for both sides. The ground the match is being played at is only fifteen minutes walk from here. Most of the people crammed in here seem to be supporters enjoying their traditional pre-match drinking session. I bet the place will empty after kick-off but we'll be long gone by then. The supporters from both sides seem to be tolerating each other but the noise in here is deafening and I feel uneasy. Maybe I'm just on edge after what happened at the concert last night. I'm worried that there's going to be trouble. Lizzie's thinking the same thing, I can see it in her face. She keeps looking around the crowd and frowning. She's noticed that I'm looking at her now and her expression has sud-denly changed.

'Okay?' she asks, trying to sound relaxed and happy but failing to convince me.

'Great,' I grunt. 'No food yet and I can't hear myself think.'

Ellis reaches across the table and tugs at my sleeve.

'Don't do that,' I snap.

'When's dinner coming?'

'When it's ready.'

'When will that be?'

'I don't know.'

'Just be patient,' Liz tells her. 'As soon as they've cooked it someone will bring it over to us.'

'I want it now,' she states, not interested in any excuses or explanations. 'I'm hungry.'

'We're all hungry, love. As soon as it's ready they'll bring it over to us and—'

'Want it now,' she says again.

'Did you hear what Mum just said?' I hiss at her, my patience rapidly wearing thin. 'Just shut up and wait. Your dinner will be here when . . .'

I stop talking. Smashing glass. There's a sudden roar of noise from deep within the crowd around the bar. I stare into the mass of faded denim and football shirts looking for trouble. I can't see anything. I'm relieved when I can hear laughs and jeers among the noise.

'What's up?' Lizzie asks me.

'Nothing,' I answer. 'Can't see anything . . .'

A very drunk, beer-soaked football fan staggers past our table on the way to the toilet. A member of the bar staff carrying a dustpan and brush passes them going the other way. Looks like it was a spilled drink, nothing more serious.

Our food finally arrives. My mouth starts watering and my stomach is growling but I can't eat yet. Another one of the joys of parenthood. Josh is sitting next to me and I now have to go through the well-rehearsed routine of cutting up his dinner and smothering it in tomato sauce before I can start mine. Both Liz and Ellis are well into their meals by the time I finally manage to pick up my knife and fork.

'Is it all right?' Liz asks me before I've finished my first mouthful. Christ, give me a second to taste it first.

'Fine,' I answer. 'Yours?'

She nods and chews.

For a blissful minute or two the table is quiet. The rest of the pub is still filled with noise but with everyone temporarily distracted by their food there's a welcome pause in our conversation. It doesn't last long.

'I want to go and see Dad tomorrow,' Lizzie says. 'That all right with you?' I nod my head as I eat. I'm not surprised. We seem to end up over at Harry's house most Sunday afternoons. We see him virtually every day now since he agreed to look after Josh so that Liz can go to work. She's a classroom assistant at the school Ed and Ellis go to. Harry's not happy about it but he does it because he knows how much we need the money.

'Okay,' I answer, finally swallowing my food, 'we'll go over in the afternoon.'

'He's been really good to us recently,' she continues. 'I don't want him to think that we're just going to keep taking.'

'Like your sister does?'

'Leave Dawn alone. She's been struggling since Mark left.'

'Best move that bloke ever made,' I say, perhaps unfairly. 'She struggled when they were together. She'll struggle whatever happens.'

'Come on, don't be unkind. It's not easy for her being on her own with the kids. I don't know how I'd cope.'

'You'd just get on with it. You'd find a way of getting by, we both would. The problem is your sister is too quick to look for the easy option all the time. What she needs is someone to—'

A sudden, unexpected and very loud clattering noise interrupts me. It's Josh. He's dropped his fork on the floor. I bend down and pick it up before cleaning it on a paper napkin and passing it back to him.

'What she needs,' Lizzie continues, taking over where I left off, 'is some space and more time to try and come to terms with what happened and what he did. She didn't deserve any of it. You can't do that to someone and then just expect them to—'

'I'm not saying she deserved anything, I just think that . . .'

Another clatter of metal on floor tile. I pick up Josh's fork for the second time, clean it and pass it back. He grins at me.

'All I'm saying is that . . .'

Josh drops his fork again. Now I'm really starting to lose my patience. I pick it up, clean it and slam it down on the table next to his plate. He squeals with laughter. Irritating little sod.

'Do that again and we're going home,' I threaten.

'Just ignore him,' Lizzie says, still managing to eat her food. I've hardly touched mine. 'He's only doing it because he's getting a reaction from you. The more you react, the more he'll do it.'

I know she's right but it's hard to keep calm. I try and concentrate on my dinner but I can feel Josh staring at me, desperate to make eye contact. I cringe as the fork hits the ground again. I know I shouldn't but I can't stop myself from reacting. I grab the fork off the floor and hold it in front of him, just out of his reach.

'Fork . . .' he whines.

'Danny . . .' Lizzie warns.

'Do you want to go home?' I hiss at him through clenched teeth. 'Or do you want to finish your dinner first? If you do that again we're going.'

'Daddy might buy you an ice cream if you finish your dinner,' Liz says.

'I might not,' I add quickly. 'Bloody hell, I've spent enough already. I can't afford to keep . . .'

There's another interruption from the crowd of football supporters. I wish they'd shut up, selfish bastards. More noise. Nervous, uncertain noise. This doesn't sound good. No-one's laughing this time. I turn round just in time to see a section of the crowd part as a squat, bald-headed and tattoo-covered man is charged across the room by another fan who seems to be about twice his height but half his weight. They've smashed into a table where another family was eating. People are up off their chairs and are scattering in all directions.

'What are they doing?' Ellis asks innocently. 'Are they playing or fighting?'

The two men are stood up again now and I'm praying they don't come any nearer. The thinner man holds the tattooed man by his jacket and he's swinging him around. He tries to grab hold of something to steady himself but the thin man's not giving him a chance. He lets him go and then runs at him and shoves him in the chest, sending him tripping backwards. Another hard shove and this time the tattooed man is pushed so far that he ends up flat on his back on another table not far from where we're sitting. Half-empty plates, cutlery and glasses are sent flying. I grab hold of Josh and I look around and see that Lizzie has done the same with Ellis. The clattering, crashing and smashing noise quickly fades away and is replaced by a heavy and uncomfortable silence. Everyone is watching the fight but it's so sudden and so violent that no-one dares to get involved. Everyone knows they should do something but no-one's moving.

'Don't, mate . . .' the man lying on his back on the table cries nervously. 'Please don't . . .'

The thin man looks around. Holding his victim down with one hand he searches through the debris on the table and picks something up. It's only when he holds it up above his head that I see he's got a steak knife. The next few seconds seem to last for ever. I don't want to watch but I can't look away. He brings the knife thumping down on the tattooed man's chest and sinks it into his flesh. But that's not enough. His fist already covered in blood he yanks the blade out then stabs it down again and again and again . . .

Fucking hell.

Christ, we have to get out of here. We have to move. This bloke's out of his mind. What if he turns on the rest of us? The hundreds of people crammed into this overcrowded pub have started to panic and are heading for the exits, running from the two men in the middle of the room. The thin man is still shredding the other man's chest with the sharp, serrated blade. The tattooed man's arms and legs are thrashing and even from this distance I can see that the table and both men are covered in blood.

I drag Josh out of his chair and then push Lizzie towards the nearest door. I'm trying hard to stay calm but I'm fucking terrified. Come on, get a fucking move on . . . There's a crowd of drinkers all trying to push their way out through a narrow doorway at the same time, and for the second time in less than a day I'm stuck at the back of a load of people trying to get away from trouble. I hold Josh close to my chest and look over my shoulder to see where the lunatic with the knife is. If he's finished with the man on the table who knows who he's going to come after next. I don't want to be his next victim. I just want to . . .

'Danny!' I hear Liz scream. I look up again. She's been pulled further along with the crowd and there are a couple of metres between us now. She's almost through the door. She's looking back and shouting something at me. I can't make it out.

'What?'

'Ed,' she yells, 'get Ed!'

Jesus Christ. There's no time to think. I hold on to Josh tightly and make a sudden change in direction back towards the fun barn. The way through is clear. The people in there can't have heard what's happening yet. I push through the swinging double doors and look around for Ed but I can't see him. The lighting is low at this end of the room and there are kids and their parents everywhere.

'Edward!' I shout over thumping party music. People turn and look at me like I've gone mad. 'Ed!'

'Dad!' I hear him shout back. I can see him now, down by one of the climbing frames at the far end of the room with a friend. I run towards him.

'Get your shoes and your coat,' I tell him, 'we've got to go.'

'But, Dad,' he starts to protest.

'Get your shoes and your coat,' I tell him again.

'What's going on?' someone asks. I turn round and see that it's Wendy Parish, the mother of one of Ed's friends.

'There's some trouble in the pub,' I tell her, watching anxiously as Ed disappears to find his stuff. 'I'd get out of here if I was you. I'd get everyone out of here.'

I look up and see that staff from the pub have reached the staff of the fun barn and they look about to make a tannoy announcement to clear the building. Ed's back with his coat on. He sits down and starts putting on his shoes.

'Come on, son,' I yell over the noise. 'Do that outside.'

Confused, he jumps up and holds onto me as we run towards the exit, weaving around the suddenly scattered tables and chairs. We push our way out into the car park and I can see Liz and Ellis standing over by the car. I run towards them. Ed hobbles along beside me, one shoe on and one shoe off. I can hear sirens approaching.

'You okay?' Liz asks.

'We're fine,' I answer, rummaging through my pockets for the keys. I open the door and between us we bundle the children inside. I gesture for her to get in and she does. I finish strapping Josh into his car seat and then get into the front and lock the door.

'Should we wait for the police?' Liz wonders, her voice little more than a whisper.

'Bollocks to that,' I answer as I start the engine and reverse quickly out of the parking bay. Cars are already queuing up to get out of the car park. 'No-one else is stopping,' I say as we join the back of the queue. 'Let's just get out of here.'

7

It's half-past nine and I've been trying to get out of Ellis's bedroom for the best part of the last hour. Poor kid's obviously been shaken up by what she saw earlier. I'm not surprised, it scared the hell out of me too. Outwardly she doesn't seem too upset but she won't stop talking about what happened. You don't know how kids are affected by seeing things like that. I've been sitting on the end of her bed answering a constant stream of questions since she shouted out for me. I've done my best but my patience is starting to wear thin. She's just milking it now, trying to keep me in here as long as she can.

'So why were they fighting, Daddy?' she asks (again).

'Ellis,' I sigh, 'I've already told you a hundred times, I don't know.'

'Have they stopped now?'

'I'm sure they have. The police would have stopped them.'

'Would they?'

'Yes, that's what the police do.'

'Did one of the men get hurt?'

'Yes.'

'Will he be in hospital now?'

'Yes,' I answer. I don't tell her that he's probably in the hospital morgue.

The questions suddenly stop. She's tired. I can see her eyelids starting to flutter. She's going to sleep but she's going to fight it all the way. I should wait until I'm sure she's gone but I'm desperate to get out of here now. I slide along the bed, get up carefully and then begin to edge towards the door. She stirs and looks up and I freeze.

'What about my chips?' she mumbles, her voice slow and drowsy.

'What about them?' I ask, moving away again.

'I didn't finish them.'

'None of us finished our food. Mummy and Daddy didn't finish either.'

'Will they still be there?'

'Will who still be there?'

'My chips.'

'I doubt it.'

'Has someone else eaten them?'

'No, they'd have gone cold by now. Someone will have thrown them away.'

'Can we go back tomorrow and see?'

'No.'

'Why not? I want to finish my chips—'

'Ellis,' I interrupt.

'What?'

'Shut up and go to sleep please.'

I've finally reached the door. I flick the light switch off and wait for her to react. She doesn't. The only light in the room now comes in from the hallway. I can still see her shuffling around in bed but I know she'll be asleep in a few minutes.

'Night, Daddy,' she yawns.

'Night, sweetheart.'

I'm about to leave when she speaks again.

'Is he dead, Daddy?'

What do I say to that? Do I tell her the truth or do I lie to save more questions and reassure my little girl? I'm a coward. I sit on the fence.

'I don't know,' I mumble quickly. 'Goodnight.'

I wait for a little while longer until I'm sure she's asleep. Finally free but exhausted I drag myself down the corridor towards the living room. Halfway through the weekend and I don't feel like I've had any chance to relax yet. There's a film on tonight that Liz and I wanted to watch. After the last couple of days it will be good just to sit down together and relax for a while.

I look around the living room door and see that Lizzie is asleep. She's sprawled out along the full length of the sofa, snoring. I'm disappointed but not surprised. I fetch myself a drink and something to eat from the kitchen before finding somewhere to sit and watch the TV. The other seats are piled high with the children's toys and clean washing waiting to be put away. I can't be bothered to move any of it. I sit down on the floor in front of the sofa.

Now I can't find the remote control. I upend most of the washing and turf through the toys but I can't find the damn thing anywhere. I bet one of the kids has hidden it. Josh has a habit of putting things in the bin. I check through the rubbish then under all the chairs and the sofa. When I'm on the verge of giving up I finally spot the end of it peeking out from underneath Lizzie. She's fallen asleep on top of it. I pull it out from under her. She grunts and rolls over onto her back but she doesn't wake up.

Just in time. Seconds to spare and I'm finally there. I change the channel and sit back to enjoy the film. Looks like it's already begun. Actually, it looks like it's been on for a while. I check the TV listings. Bloody thing started three-quarters of an hour ago.

Saturday nights are beginning to depress me. For a while now they've begun to feel empty and, if I'm honest, pathetic. We're still young and we should be out enjoying ourselves but we're not. I always start the weekend with the best of intentions but things never seem to work out how I planned them. Family life gets in the way. I don't have many close friends to go out with or any spare money, the kids wind us up and wear us out and Lizzie and I are both tired all the time. More often than not I'm left sitting here on my own like this in front of the TV watching pointless drivel. It's almost midnight now and I've wasted hours here on my own. Liz got up and went to bed ages ago.

The film I missed was the only thing worth watching tonight. It's crazy – the more TV channels we get, the fewer programmes worth watching there are. I've been sat here with the remote control in my hand constantly flicking through the channels and all I've found has been terrible game shows, chat shows with boring guests, pointless reality TV programmes, soap operas, talent competitions, made-for-TV films, repeated dramas and crappy compilations of CCTV footage and home video clips. I've ended up watching the news as usual. It's a rolling twenty-four-hour news channel which was interesting for a while but the headlines are on a fifteen-minute loop and my eyes are starting to feel heavy now that I'm watching the same thing for the third time. I should go to bed but I can't be bothered to get up.

Hold on a minute. Finally there's something moderately interesting on screen. A banner saying 'Breaking News' has just appeared and they've cut to a reporter standing on a city centre street corner. I recognise where they're broadcasting from. It's a place in town, not far from where I work. What's happened there? I try to read the scrolling text captions at the bottom of the screen but my eyes are tired and the words are moving too quickly. I turn up the volume and listen as a windswept reporter starts talking about something that's happened at Exodus, one of the trendy bars right in the centre of town. There are people milling around in the street behind him. Christ, someone's been killed. He's talking about an attack that happened in the last hour or so. Hold on, no . . . there have been several attacks. They must have been connected. Sounds like some lunatic has gone on the rampage. Worst time of the week for it to have happened. The middle of town is always heaving with people on Saturday nights. Everyone's there. Everyone except sad bastards like me, that is, stuck at home with the kids and a partner who's asleep by half-past nine.

I can feel my eyes starting to close again. I try to stay awake and concentrate on what's being said but it's difficult. It's getting late and . . .

That bloody reporter is still talking.

I try and focus on the clock on the shelf. I must have nodded off for a few minutes. Hang on, the clock says three-thirty. I've been asleep on the floor for hours. No wonder my bones ache. Christ, whatever happened in town tonight must have been pretty serious to warrant this much coverage on national TV. It looks like they're still broadcasting live from town. I wouldn't want to have that bloke's job, stuck out on a street corner for hours on end. Still, at least he gets out . . .

My back hurts. I should have gone to bed hours ago when Lizzie did.

I sit up quickly and get ready to move. I hate waking up like this. I feel sick and my arms and legs feel heavy and numb. I get up and I'm about to switch the TV off when something the reporter says makes me stop. He's not just talking about the same few attacks he was reporting on earlier. Sounds like there's been more trouble. There's a map of the city up on the screen now with a load of markers on it. Looks like there's been a hell of a lot more trouble. That's the problem with binge drinking and Saturday nights. There are so many people out there and it only takes one idiot to start a fight. Someone gets hurt then someone retaliates, someone else tries to stop them and, before you know it, you've got a real problem on your hands. It looks like that's what's happened tonight. From what I can gather there was some trouble in a bar which spilled out onto the street. They're showing footage of crowds of people fighting now, fuelled by drink and drugs. Riot police have been sent to the scene to try and restore some order. Almost makes me glad to be boring and stuck indoors. The map on the screen has been updated now to show the location of four fatalities and more than thirty arrests. It's always the mindless minority who ruin it for everyone else. Bloody hell, they've just said something about the body of a police officer that's been found with more than forty stab wounds. Christ, what kind of animal could do that to another human being?

Wonder how long that reporter's going to be stuck out there?

I'm tired. Before I fall asleep again I switch off the TV and the lights and feel my way through the dark flat to the bedroom.

SUNDAY

iv

Susan Myers woke up next to Charlie, her husband of thirty-three years. She lay in silence in the semi-darkness, taking care not to move. She didn't want him to know that she was awake. She didn't want to have to speak to him. Through half-open eyes she watched the curtain as it gusted back and forth in the wind from the vented window, revealing snatched glimpses of the bright world outside. Was there any point in getting up? During the week she managed to fill her time with friends, shopping and social appointments but her weekends, Sundays in particular, were long, bleak and empty. Since Charlie had retired eleven months ago their lives had become increasingly dull and monotonous. Most of her friends had their children and extended families to keep them busy but all she had was him and he bored her. He seemed happy doing nothing but she couldn't stand it. He wanted to potter around the house and garden, she wanted to be out. She wanted to scream and shout at him and make him understand how she felt but she knew it would be pointless. He didn't even know she was unhappy.

Here we go, she thought as he shuffled and turned over in bed beside her. Maybe – just maybe – he'd roll over to face her this morning and put his arm around her tell her that he loved her and start kissing her and touching her like he used to. It had been so long since they'd made love that she'd almost forgotten what it felt like. And on the very rare occasions she'd managed to get him in the mood (she was always the one who had to make the first move these days) he'd get himself so fired up and over-excited that their passion, if it could be called that, was generally over and done with in a matter of a few desperately short and empty minutes. If it had been months since they'd made love, it had been years since she'd been satisfied.

Maybe she should have an affair? She'd thought about it before but never had the nerve to do it. Charlie probably wouldn't notice *if she did. There was a man at one of the mid-week dancing classes she went to who she'd caught looking in her direction too many times for it to have just been coincidence. The idea of seeing someone else tempted her, but she knew she'd be putting a lot at risk if she ever actually did it. She was worried that she might end up losing everything she'd worked for with Charlie just for a little short-term excitement and adventure. She loved her grand house and her expensive clothes and all the associated trimmings. She loved the elevated social status it gave her and she didn't want to let any of it go. But what if the man at the dance class could give her all that and sex too . . . ?*

'Cup of tea?'

That was how Charlie started every day. No 'good morning' or 'how are you today?' or 'I love you' or anything like that any more. Just a short, unemotional, truncated question. Should she answer or should she stay silent and pretend to still be asleep?

'Yes please,' she grunted, still with her back to her husband. She felt him throw back the covers and then slide out of bed before neatly tucking the bedding back into place again as he always did. Everything he did was predictable and safe. She could anticipate every move he was going to make. She knew he'd go to the bathroom next where he'd use the toilet, break wind, apologise to himself and then wash and shave humming the same damn tune he hummed under his breath every bloody morning. Then he'd put on his dressing gown, come back to the bedroom to fetch his slippers from under the foot of the bed where he'd put them the night before, and go down to the kitchen. She knew he'd stop on the fifth step down to open the curtains and blow the dust off the top of the employee of the year trophy his employers had awarded him almost fifteen years ago . . .

She screwed her eyes tightly shut, buried her face in the duvet and thought of the man from the dance class again. She felt empty and depressed, trapped and angry. Sometimes she wanted to kill her husband. That, she decided, would be the answer to all her problems.

'Lovely day today,' Charlie said brightly as he returned to the bedroom with two cups of tea.

'It's always a bloody lovely day,' Susan silently screamed to herself. 'Even when it's raining and there's a force ten gale outside he says it's a bloody lovely day.'

'Here's your tea, dear.'

She cringed under the bedclothes and readied herself to face him. Saddest thing of all, she thought, was that he didn't have the faintest idea how unhappy she was. In his rose-tinted little world everything was just fine and dandy. He didn't know how old and worthless he made her feel and he probably never would. She took a deep breath and rolled over onto her back before shuffling up the bed and taking her tea from him.

'I had a lousy night's sleep,' she complained, looking up at him. 'I was freezing cold all night. I kept waking up because you kept pulling the covers off me.'

'Sorry about that, my love. I didn't realise.'

'And if it wasn't the cold keeping me awake it was your snoring.'

'I can't help that. If there was something I could do to . . .'

He stopped talking. In silence he stared down at his wife who scowled back at him.

'What's the matter with you?' she demanded as she sipped her tea.

Charlie continued to stare.

'For crying out loud, find something else to look at will you?' she cursed before taking another sip.

With a single sudden swipe Charlie slapped the cup out of his wife's hands. It smashed against the wall opposite sending countless dribbles of tea dripping down the pale pink Anaglypta wallpaper. Bemused, Susan watched the drips of hot brown liquid trickling down the wall. What the hell's got into him? she wondered. In a bizarre way she was actually excited by this sudden display of unexpected forcefulness and spontaneity.

Behind her Charlie quickly yanked the waist belt free from his towelling dressing gown. Shoving her forward and gripping her shoulder tight with one hand he looped the belt twice round her neck in a single spiralling movement and then pulled it tight. Panicking, and with her eyes bulging and throat burning, Susan struggled to breathe. She kicked and squirmed under the bedclothes *and scraped at her neck, desperately trying to force her fingers under the belt. Her strength was no match for his.*

Charlie pulled the belt tighter and tighter until the last breath had been squeezed from his wife's body.

8

Another bloody wasted day.

Today started slowly. I got out of bed late (which really annoyed Lizzie – she had to get up and see to the kids for once) and I made a conscious effort to do as little as possible. I'm back at work tomorrow and I need to relax. I tried hard to do nothing but it's impossible in this house. There's always something to do or someone who needs you. Liz has been nagging at me for weeks to fix the bolt on the bathroom door and, today, I finally did it. It was the last thing I wanted to do but I reached the point where I couldn't stand her complaining about it every single time she used the damn toilet. Christ, the rest of us managed without any problems. Why was it such a big deal for her?

I worked on the door as Lizzie cooked dinner. What should have been a ten-minute job ended up taking over an hour and a half. I had the kids running round my feet the whole time asking questions and getting in the way, then I didn't have the right size bolt, then I bought one that was too big . . . I lost my temper and almost kicked the door in but I finally fixed it. Hope Lizzie's satisfied. She'll have to find something else to complain about now.

And now here we are approaching Harry's house and the weekend's almost over. I genuinely don't mind Harry but he seems to have a huge problem with me. He doesn't think I'm good enough for his little girl and although he never says it as blatantly as that it's implied in just about everything he says to me. I can usually just shrug it off but when the day has been as frustrating as today and Monday morning is looming on the horizon it's something I could well do without.

We pull up outside his narrow terraced house and the kids start to get wound up and excited. They enjoy their time with Grandpa. Truth is they tolerate their time with Harry. They put up with it because they know they'll get sweets or some other treat out of him before they go home.

'I don't want any arguing today,' Liz says as we wait for him to answer the front door. I think she's talking to the kids but I realise she's looking at me.

'I never argue with your dad,' I tell her. 'He argues with me. There's a difference you know.'

'I'm not interested,' she says as the latch clicks open. 'Just be nice.'

The door opens inwards. Harry opens his arms to the kids and they run towards him, giving him a dutiful squeeze before disappearing deeper inside to trash his house.

'Hello, love,' he says to Lizzie as she hugs him.

'You okay, Dad?'

'Fine,' he smiles. 'Better now. I've been looking forward to seeing you lot all day.'

Lizzie follows the children into the house. I go inside, wipe my feet and shut the door behind me.

'Harry,' I say, acknowledging him. I don't mean to sound abrupt but I unintentionally do.

'Daniel,' he replies, equally abruptly. He turns and walks towards the kitchen. 'I'll put the kettle on.'

I step over the children (who are already sprawled out across the living room floor) and head for my usual spot – the armchair in the corner of the room near the back window. I grab the Sunday newspapers off the coffee table as I pass. Burying my head in Harry's papers always helps me get through these long and monotonous visits.

A couple of minutes go by before Harry reappears with a tray of drinks. Vile, milky tea for Liz and me and equally weak, over-diluted fruit juice for the children. I take my tea from him.

'Thanks,' I say quietly. He doesn't acknowledge me. He hardly even looks at me.

I sit down in the corner of the room and start to read. I'm not interested in the politics or the finance or the travel or the style and fashion sections. I head straight for the cartoons. That's about the level I can cope with today.

We've been here for almost an hour and I've hardly said a word. Lizzie's been dozing on the sofa on the other side of the room and Harry has been sitting on the floor with the kids. There's no disputing the fact that they get on well together. He's laughing and joking with them and they're loving it. Makes me feel like a bad parent if I'm honest. I don't enjoy being with the children like he does. Maybe it's because he can walk away from them and we can't. They drain me, and I know Lizzie feels the same too. Everything's an effort when you have kids.

'Grandpa just made a coin disappear!' Ellis squeals, tugging at my trouser leg. Harry fancies himself as something of an amateur magician. He's always making things disappear and reappear. She squeals again as he 'magically' finds the coin tucked behind her ear. It doesn't take much to impress a four-year-old . . .

'Your Uncle Keith's gone into hospital again,' Harry says, turning around to speak to Lizzie who stirs and sits up.

'How's Annie coping?' she asks, covering her mouth with her hand as she yawns. I don't bother listening to Harry's answer. I've never met Liz's Uncle Keith or Auntie Annie and I don't suppose I ever will. I feel like I know them though, the number of times I've had to sit here and listen to endless trivial stories about their empty lives on the other side of the country. This happens most Sunday afternoons. Liz and Harry start talking about families and reminiscing and I just switch off. They'll talk constantly now until we go home about people I've never heard of and places I've never been.

'Mind if I put the football on?' I ask, noticing the time and stumbling on a way of keeping myself awake. Both Harry and Lizzie look up, surprised that I've spoken.

'Carry on,' grumbles Harry. He makes it sound as if watching the match will stop him talking or prevent him from doing something more important. Truth is he likes football as much as I do. I switch on the TV and the room is suddenly filled with noise. I swear he's going deaf. The volume's almost at maximum. I turn it down and I'm about to change channels when I stop.

'Bloody hell,' I say under my breath.

'What's the matter?' asks Liz.

'Have you seen this?'

I point at the screen. It's the same news channel I was watching last night. It's the same story too. The violence I'd seen reported appears to have continued to spread. It looks like a wave of trouble has washed right across our town. Although it looks quieter now the screen shows pictures of damaged buildings and rubbish-filled streets.

'I saw this earlier,' Harry says. 'It's a bloody disgrace if you ask me.'

'What's happened?' asks Liz.

'Haven't you seen any news yet today?'

'You know what it's like in our house, Dad,' she replies as she shuffles around to get a better view of the screen. 'We're last on the list when it comes to choosing what we watch on TV.'

'You want to start putting your foot down,' he moans, looking directly at me, trying to get me to bite. 'Show them you're in charge. You should never let children rule the roost like that.'

I ignore him and answer Liz.

'There was some trouble last night,' I explain. 'I saw it before I went to bed. There were a few incidents around town that got out of control.'

'What do you mean, got out of control?'

'You know what it's like in town on a Saturday. If there's a night when things will kick off it will always be Saturday. The streets are filled with idiots who are pissed up and off their faces on drugs. The police can't cope with them as it is. Apparently it all started with a fight in a bar that got out of hand. More and more people got involved and it turned into a riot.'

'Grandpa, we saw a fight yesterday,' Ellis says innocently, looking up from her colouring book. Harry looks at Liz who nods her head.

'It was horrible, Dad,' she explains. 'We took Ed to a party at the King's Head. It was full of football fans. We were having a meal and two of them started fighting.' She stops speaking and checks that the children aren't listening. 'One of them had a knife,' she says, her voice a little lower.

Harry shakes his head.

'It's a sad state of affairs, it really is,' he sighs. 'It's almost as if people go out looking for trouble these days.

The room falls quiet momentarily.

'Hang on,' Lizzie says suddenly, 'did you say this trouble happened here?'

'Yes,' I answer, nodding my head, 'why?'

'Because this is talking about somewhere else,' she says, nodding towards the TV. She's right. This report is coming from another place further north, and now they've cut to a third reporter on the east coast.

'It's mob violence,' Harry chunters. 'It spreads. People see something on TV and it makes them want to go out and do the same.'

He might be right but I doubt it very much. This doesn't make sense. I can't imagine that these people are all fighting just for the sake of it. There must be a reason.

'There must be more to it than that,' I say. 'For Christ's sake, Harry, do you really believe these people were just sat watching the trouble on TV one minute and then were out on the streets fighting the next? These riots are hundreds of miles apart. There must be more to it.'

For once he doesn't answer.

Another twenty minutes and the children have reached and exceeded their boredom threshold. They've started playing up and it's time to leave. I try to hide my relief as I bundle them into the back of the car. They bicker and fight constantly and I wonder if they're as wound up about Monday morning as I am. I hate Sunday evenings. All that's left now is the rush to get everything ready for school and work tomorrow.

This is the worst part of the weekend. Nothing to look forward to now except Monday.

9

We're still half a mile from home and I don't know what the hell is going on. The traffic has suddenly slowed. It's backed up as far as I can see both ahead of us and behind and we're hardly moving. It's Sunday evening, for Christ's sake. The roads should be empty. It's already getting dark. I don't want to spend the whole night sat here.

I can hear sirens. I look into the rear-view mirror and I can see a mass of flashing blue lights coming up on us at speed. A convoy of police cars and fire engines are approaching from behind and there are more flashing lights coming the other way too. The drivers of the cars around us shuffle to the side and mount the pavement to get out of the way. I do the same.

'Wonder what's happened,' Liz mumbles as we bump up onto the grass verge.

'Don't know,' I answer. There's a noise from the back seat and I look around to see Ed and Ellis fighting with each other across Josh who's trapped in his baby seat. 'Cut it out,' I snap angrily. They stop when I tell them but I know they'll start again the second I look away.

The emergency vehicles rumble past us and I crane my neck to watch where they go. They take a left-hand turn a couple of hundred yards ahead. In the semi-darkness I can see the blinking blue lights through the gaps between buildings and the branches of trees. They've stopped not far from here.

'Looks serious, doesn't it?' Lizzie says, keeping her voice quiet so the children don't hear.

The traffic is at a complete standstill now and it looks like people have turned off their engines. Some are starting to get out of their cars. I can't stand sitting behind the wheel if I'm not going anywhere. I decide to go and have a look too. I'll try and see how long we're likely to be stuck here.

'Back in a second,' I say as I switch off the engine and undo my seat belt.

'What are you doing?'

'Just going to see what's happening,' I answer quickly.

'Can I come?' Ed asks. I turn to face him as I climb out of the car.

'No, you wait here. I'll only be a minute.'

He slouches back in his seat and scowls.

Lizzie's not happy being left with the kids but I go anyway. I follow a group of three people from the car in front of us around the corner. There's a large crowd gathering in the next street. As I get closer I can see that a dark blue estate car has lost control and mounted the pavement. It's hit a street lamp which has fallen onto the front drive of a house and destroyed a caravan which was parked there. The police are trying to cordon off the scene. They're pushing people back but I manage to keep moving forward until I'm right at the front of the crowd. The car's a total write-off. Its bonnet is smashed and crumpled and the driver is slumped against the steering wheel. He's not moving. The fire brigade are setting up their cutting equipment to get him out but no-one's rushing. Looks like they're already too late.

There are two paramedics and a police officer crouching down at the front of the car. Has someone else been injured too? One of the green-suited medical officers gets up to fetch something. Bloody hell, there's a body under the car. I can't see much, just a twisted, broken leg sticking out from under what's left of the bonnet at an awkward angle. Poor sod. Whoever it was they didn't stand a chance.

I stand and stare at the crash scene until the police decide to widen their cordon again and I'm pushed further back. I realise I've left Lizzie on her own for too long and I quickly turn and start to walk back towards the car. I stumble into a man walking his dog when he stops suddenly as the dog veers off to the left towards the hedge.

'Sorry, mate,' I mumble quickly.

'You're all right,' he replies as he tries to yank the dog back out of my way. The dog isn't responding. 'Come on, boy,' he snaps.

'Nasty accident, that,' I say.

He shakes his head.

'That wasn't an accident.'

'What?'

He looks into my face and shakes his head again.

'I saw the whole thing happen,' he tells me. 'Bloody idiot.'

'Who?'

'The bloke driving the car. Absolute bloody idiot.'

'Why?'

'First thing I know is when some lad runs past me,' he explains. 'Came out of nowhere, he did, nearly knocked me flying. Then the car comes past and drives onto the pavement just up from where I'm walking. The lad's running as fast as he can but there's nothing he can do. The driver puts his foot down and just accelerates and runs him over and drives straight into the wall. Stupid bastard. Looks like he's killed himself too.'

The man finally moves his dog out of the way and I start to walk forward again, trying to make sense of what I've just heard. This weekend has been full of bizarre and horrific events. First the concert, then the attack in the pub yesterday and now this. And there was the man in the street on Thursday morning too. I think back to the news report we were watching at Harry's house. What the hell is going on?

MONDAY

V

Ten *times the trouble wouldn't have kept some drinkers away. The club was emptier than usual but these were the hardened few – the regular drinkers and clubbers who wouldn't miss a night out no matter what they'd seen on the news or read in the papers. For these people the rest of the week revolved around nights like this. Getting pissed, getting stoned and getting laid was all that mattered.*

'She's fucking gorgeous, mate,' Shane White yelled into Newbury's ear. 'She keeps looking at you. Get in there, son!'

Newbury turned to White and grinned.

'Reckon I'm in with a chance then?'

'No fucking problem. She's yours, mate, no question.'

'Serious?'

'Serious.'

'Right then. Watch this.'

Newbury pushed himself away from the bar, knocked back the last of his drink and stood and watched her. He didn't even know her name. He'd seen her here a few times before but she'd always been surrounded by blokes and her friends and he'd never had the nerve to try anything with her. It felt different tonight. He felt confident and alive. Maybe he felt less intimidated because there were fewer people around? Maybe it was just because he was already half-drunk. Whatever the reason it didn't matter. Fucking hell, he thought as he watched her dance, Shane's right, she's fucking gorgeous. He slowly walked towards her and she began to dance towards him.

'You all right?' he shouted, fighting to make himself heard over the thumping music which filled the half-empty club. It seemed louder than ever in here tonight with fewer people around. She didn't answer. Instead she just beckoned him closer, wrapped her arms around him and shoved her tongue down his throat.

*

'You're bloody beautiful, you are,' Newbury babbled breathlessly as they left the club and walked together towards an alley opposite the town hall. 'Absolutely bloody beautiful.'

'Are you going to spend all night talking or what?' she asked as she led him into the shadows. He couldn't answer. 'I could have stayed at home if I wanted to talk. All I need from you is a good, hard fuck.'

Newbury struggled to believe what he was hearing. He'd never had this happen before. He'd fantasised about it enough times and he'd heard about it happening to other people, but it had never actually happened to him. And he'd never dreamt it might happen with a girl like this . . .

She stopped walking and turned towards him, pushing her body against his. She ripped open his shirt.

'Here?' he asked. 'You dirty bitch . . . !'

'This is how I like it,' she hissed in his ear. He could smell the booze on her breath. Somehow that made it more sordid and more exciting.

Newbury was in danger of becoming too fired up and turned on to perform. Staying in control was getting more difficult every time she touched him or kissed him or . . . she pushed him back hard against the wall and kissed him again, chewing on his lips and forcing her tongue deep into his mouth. He shoved his hand down the back of her skirt and pulled her even closer. In response she undid his trouser zip, slid her hand inside and slipped her fingers around his drunken erection. She held it firmly but gently and teased it out of his trousers and towards her.

'Get your knickers off,' he gasped in a momentary pause between frantic bites and kisses.

'What knickers?' she whispered in his ear as she hitched her tight skirt up around her waist. Still locked together they rolled to the side until she was the one with her back to the wall. 'Come on,' she moaned, desperate for him, 'give it to me.'

Newbury shuffled into position and tried to slide into her. It was awkward and rough. The booze had affected both of their coordination. She gasped with sudden pleasure as his full length finally disappeared inside her.

'I'll give it to you, you dirty slut,' he promised as he forced himself deeper still. She looked up to the sky and bit her lip, trying

*not to make any noise but at the same time desperate to scream out
loud.*

'Harder,' she hissed.

*He began to thrust his body against hers, forcing her back
against the wall again and again.*

*'Hard enough for you?' he asked, staring deep into her wide grey
eyes.*

'Just fuck me,' she gasped between thrusts.

'Hard enough?' he hissed again through clenched teeth.

Then she stopped.

She let go of him.

*'What's the matter?' he asked, concerned. 'Did I hurt you? What
did I do?'*

*The expression on her face changed from pleasure to fear in an
instant. She pushed him off and backed away from him, pulling her
skirt down and tripping back across the alley.*

'What's going on?' he asked again. 'What's the matter with you?'

*She didn't answer. She kept moving away, shuffling deeper into
the shadows. He continued to move towards her. She tried to speak
but she couldn't. 'Don't . . .' was all she could mumble.*

*'What the fucking hell's going on?' he demanded. 'You're
mental, you are. One minute you're all over me, now you're pushing me away. Is this how you get your kicks? You're a fucking
prick-teaser. You're a dirty fucking bitch.'*

*Still staggering backwards her foot kicked against the edge of a
plastic crate filled with empty glass bottles. She instinctively leant
down, picked up one of the bottles by its neck and smashed it
against the brick wall behind her.*

His reactions dulled by drink, Newbury stood and watched her.

*'Now what are you doing? You're fucking crazy, you are. What
the fucking hell do you think you're doing? I'm not . . .'*

*He didn't finish his sentence. She ran at him and shoved the
broken bottle deep into his stomach. It sliced through his cotton
shirt and plunged into his flesh. She pulled the bottle out and then
shoved it into him again, this time lower, the jagged edge almost
severing the bottom third of his still exposed but now completely
flaccid penis. Then a third strike as she sunk the razor-sharp glass
into his neck.*

She turned and ran and was out of the alley before he'd hit the ground.

There were more of them out there, thousands more.

She had to keep running.

10

Sometimes the thought of work is worse than the reality. All things considered, today at the office was just about bearable. After everything I'd seen and heard over the weekend I'd expected to have to fight my way into work through crowds of people battling with each other on the streets. Apart from a few broken windows and some other slight damage everything looked and felt disappointingly normal. The city centre was quiet for a Monday and the office was too.

I'm glad to be home. I can see the apartment block at the end of the road now. As usual there are lights on in the diagonally opposite corners of the building – our flat and the other occupied flat upstairs. As I get closer I can see shadows moving around behind our curtains. The kids are running around in the living room. No doubt they'll have been playing up all evening and I'll get it in the neck from Liz again.

We shouldn't be living in a place like this I think as I walk up the overgrown pathway to the door. I know I'm a lazy sod and I should work harder but it's not easy. I do my best, it's just that it doesn't seem to be enough. I need a kick up the backside from time to time. But if every day could be like today, I decide as I pull open the creaking front door, then maybe things might work out. Today it actually felt like the effort I'd put in had been worthwhile. I didn't have any screaming members of the public to deal with and I even managed to have a laugh with Tina Murray. Today, for once, I didn't feel as if I was pulling in the opposite direction to everyone else. The plans that Lizzie and I have been making for years to move to a bigger house, change the car and generally improve our standard of living seem a little more realistic and possible than they did when I left the flat this morning. Still a long way off, mind, but possible.

I shuffle though the gloom of the lobby and open the door to the flat. I step inside and the warmth of our home makes me realise just how cold it is outside tonight.

'I'm back,' I shout as I take off my coat and shoes. It's unusually quiet in here. I can hear the TV and the children but I can't hear Liz. She's usually yelling at one of them. I can't remember the last time I came home and it was this quiet.

Edward appears in the hallway in front of me. He's grinning from ear to ear.

'Okay, Ed?'

He nods his head.

'Had half a day off today,' he beams, looking pleased with himself.

'Why, what's the matter with you?'

'Nothing. School was shut.'

'Why?' I ask again as I walk further into the flat, looking for Liz. I can't see her in any of the bedrooms.

'Because of Jack Foster,' Ed explains. I'm confused.

'Who's Jack Foster?'

'He's in Year Six. You should have seen him, Dad, it was brilliant!'

I've reached the kitchen door. I can see Lizzie in there sitting at the table, drinking a cup of coffee and staring into space.

'You okay?' I ask. She looks up, surprised.

'Didn't know you were back,' she says quietly, shaking herself out of her trance. She gets up, walks over to me and hugs me. This sudden display of affection is out of character.

'What's that for?' I whisper, my mouth pressed close to her ear. 'You all right?'

She nods then pushes herself away and goes to fetch my dinner from the oven.

'I'm fine,' she sighs. 'Had a bad day, that's all.'

'Ed was telling me that the school was closed. Something to do with Jack Foster?'

She puts my food down on the table and sits in a chair opposite to the place she's laid for me. I start to eat and watch as she massages her temples. She looks tired and upset. I'm assuming that whatever happened at school today is what's bothering her.

'So what happened?' I ask. She doesn't want to answer. 'Talk to me, Liz . . .'

She clears her throat and finishes her coffee. When she finally starts to speak her voice is quiet and full of emotion.

'Do you know Jack Foster?'

I shake my head. I've heard the name before but I can't place the face.

'You know Ben Paris? Short lad with black hair?'

I'm sure I know who Ben is.

'His dad's the hairdresser?'

'That's the one. Jack Foster is his best friend. They're always hanging around together. We sat next to Jack's mum Sally at parents evening last term. He's got a sister in Ed's class. He's tall and . . .'

'. . . and he wears glasses?'

'That's him.'

I'm pretty sure I know who she's talking about. I say that I do just to keep the conversation moving.

'So what did he do?'

Lizzie clears her throat again and composes herself.

'First thing this morning,' she begins, 'the whole school was in the hall for assembly. The kids were crammed into the middle of the hall and Mrs Shields was parading up and down doing her usual routine at the front.'

'I can't stand that woman,' I interrupt. Mrs Shields is the head-teacher. By all accounts she's strict and old-fashioned and she speaks to the parents in exactly the same way as she speaks to the kids.

'I know you don't like her,' Liz sighs, 'you tell me every time I mention her name. Anyway, she was just finishing off one of her bloody awful Bible stories. I was sat at the back next to Denise Jones and . . .'

She stops speaking and I stop eating. I look up from my dinner and put down my knife and fork.

'And . . . ?'

'Jack's in Year Six,' she continues. 'The children sit on the floor in age order with the youngest at the front so Jack's class was at the back of the hall near where we were. Mrs Shields had just asked them to bow their heads for the final prayer before lessons . . .'

She stops again.

'So what happened?' I press.

'I was sat there at the back and Jack stood up right in front of me. Most of the children were in front of him and they all had their heads down so there wasn't much of a reaction at first. Then he just started to run towards Mrs Shields. He was kicking and tripping over the kids and some of them got hurt and started to shout and squeal. By the time everyone had looked up Jack had made it over to the side of the hall. He shoved Eileen Callis off her chair and she ended up flat on her face on the floor. All this happened in seconds. We were all just sat there, too surprised to do anything. Jack grabbed hold of Eileen's empty chair, lifted it up over his head and ran at Mrs Shields. She moved towards him to try and stop him but he was running at her, swinging the chair round over his head and just missing the kids sitting down at the front. He missed her a couple of times but then he hit her right across her face, just under her eye. Jack's almost as tall as Mrs Shields. He kept swinging the chair at her and before anyone knew what was happening she was lying flat on the floor with him standing over her, smashing the chair down on her back again and again.'

'Didn't anyone stop him?' I ask.

'Don Collingwood and Judith Lamb got to him first,' she answers, nodding. 'Don grabbed him and Judith tried to wrestle the chair off him. Bloody hell, Danny, it was like he was possessed or something. It was horrible. Mrs Shields was screaming and that was making some of the kids scream. She was curled up in a ball on the floor next to the piano with her hands over her head. Her hair was all over the place and her glasses were smashed. She had blood running down her face and . . .'

'But why?' I interrupt. 'What was the matter with him?'

She shrugs.

'Nothing as far as I know. I saw him before school started and he seemed fine. He was having a laugh with his mates. I've never known him do anything like this. There are plenty of kids at that school who wouldn't have surprised me if they'd done it, but not Jack . . .'

'Doesn't make any sense,' I mumble, my mouth full of food.

'You're telling me.'

'So what did they do with him?'

She shakes her head.

'The place went crazy. Don dragged Jack off into one of the

offices and locked him in. He trashed the place. He was screaming and shouting and . . . and God, it was horrible. The poor kid, you could hear him right the way through the school. He sounded terrified.'

'What about the Head? What about Mrs Shields?'

'They took her to hospital and had her checked over. I think she was okay, just a few cuts and bruises, that's all.'

I turn my attention back to my food for a second but it's impossible not to keep thinking about what Liz has told me.

'What made him do it?' I ask, knowing full well that she won't be able to answer.

'No idea,' she sighs, getting up to make another drink. 'Makes you wonder if it's connected to what we saw over the weekend.'

'Can't be,' I snap instinctively. 'This was a kid at a school, how could it be connected?'

'I don't know. Anyway, they closed the school not long after it happened and it's probably going to be closed again tomorrow. We tried to keep the kids distracted but you know what it's like, Dan, it's a small school. It's a close school. Everyone knows everybody else. They had to call the police in to deal with him in the end. Christ, I felt so sorry for Sally. You should have seen her. She looked like she was the one who'd done wrong. And when they took Jack away . . .'

'When who took him away?'

'They took him off in an ambulance in the end. He wouldn't speak to Sally, wouldn't even look at her. He was screaming for help. Poor kid had lost it completely. He didn't have a clue what he was doing. Wouldn't let anyone near him. It was like he was scared of the rest of us.'

11

It's past ten o'clock before we know it. The children are finally settled and asleep and the flat is silent. The television has been off all evening but now the living room is too quiet so I switch it on just so that we have some background noise. Liz is subdued and preoccupied and we've hardly talked. It's getting late. It won't be long before we go to bed. Before we know it I'll be up again and back into the grind. Sometimes I feel like I'm running at a different speed to the rest of the world. I feel like I'm always having to go flat out just to keep up.

I go to the kitchen and make us both a drink. I take Lizzie's through to her.

'Drink.'

She looks up and smiles and takes the cup from me.

'You okay?' I ask.

'Of course I am. Why do you keep asking me if I'm okay?'

'Just want to be sure you're all right. You've had a shitty day.'

'I have but I'm okay,' she says, her voice a little edgy and tense.

'Fine,' I grumble, overreacting, 'sorry I asked.'

'Oh come on, don't be like that . . .'

'Be like what? I only asked if you were okay, that's all.'

I sit down next to her. She stretches out her arm behind me and begins to gently rub my back.

'Sorry.'

'Doesn't matter.'

Same old rubbish on TV. I pick up the remote and work my way through the channels. The comedies aren't funny tonight and the dramas are too dramatic. Nothing seems to suit the mood. I head for the news. I want to find out more about what's been going on. Apart from hearing the odd snippet of information at work today this is the first chance I've had all day to catch up. What we see is more of what we saw yesterday – more trouble and more violence. What we don't get is any explanation. Each individual report seems

86

to follow a pretty standard format – one or more incidents take place in a particular area and they report how people react to the fall-out. This is insane. I keep hearing phrases like 'copycat violence' and 'revenge attacks' being bandied around. Are people really as stupid as Harry tried to suggest yesterday? Would anyone really want to start trouble just because they've seen others doing it?

'Look at that,' Lizzie says as we stare at the headlines together, 'they're even giving them a name now. How's that going to help?'

She's right. I heard the word used a few minutes earlier but didn't think anything of it. The minority who are causing the trouble have been branded 'Haters'. It came from a tabloid news-paper headline that was published this morning and it's quickly stuck. It seems appropriate because there's still no mention of these people fighting for any cause or reason. Hate seems to be just about the only thing driving them.

'They have to give them a name,' I mumble. 'It makes it easier for them to talk about it if they give them a name.'

Lizzie shakes her head in disbelief.

'I don't understand any of this.'

'Nor me.'

'They're talking about it like it's an epidemic. How can it be? It's not a disease, for Christ's sake.'

'It might be.'

'I doubt it. But there has to be a reason for all of it, doesn't there?'

She's right, but like everyone else I have no idea what that reason might be so I don't bother answering. Watching the news makes me feel increasingly uneasy. It's making me feel like shutting the front door and not opening it again until all of this sudden violence and disruption has stopped. I instinctively start trying to come up with an explanation to try and make myself feel better if nothing else.

'Maybe it's not as bad as they're making it out to be,' I suggest.

'What?'

'They always exaggerate things on the TV, don't they? They've just been saying something about an increase in the number of violent incidents being reported, but that doesn't necessarily mean there's been any increase in the number of incidents actually taking place, does it?'

'Not necessarily,' she says, sounding unsure.

'There might have been just as many fights as last week, but they weren't newsworthy then. Problem is when something like this makes the headlines people start jumping on the bandwagon.'

'What are you saying?'

'Maybe this whole situation is something the TV and newspapers have created,' I say. I'm making this up as I'm going along.

'It can't be. Something's definitely happening out there. There are too many coincidences for—'

'Okay,' I interrupt, 'but if they haven't created the problem they're definitely making it worse.'

'What about what happened at the concert on Friday? And in the pub? And whatever was going on with that car last night and what happened at school this morning . . . are you saying that all those things would have happened anyway? Do you think we're reading more into them just because of what we've seen on TV?'

'I don't know. There's no way of telling, is there? All I'm saying is that we've seen things like this get out of control before.'

'Have we?'

'Of course we have. It happens all the time. Someone somewhere broadcasts a story, then a brain-dead section of the audience copy just to try and get themselves on TV or on the front pages of the papers.'

Now I think I've really lost her. I can tell from the expression on her face that she doesn't understand. Either that or she doesn't believe me. I'm not entirely sure about this myself.

'Don't get you.'

'Remember dangerous dogs?' I ask. She shakes her head and screws up her face again. 'A few years back a kid round here got attacked by their neighbour's pet Rottweiler, remember? The kid's face got all messed up and she needed surgery I think. They had the dog put down.'

'So? What's that got to do with what's happening now?'

'Point is until that story broke hardly anyone had heard anything about dogs attacking kids, had they? But as soon as it made the papers there were suddenly stories about the same thing happening all over the place. There was a bloody epidemic of dogs attacking kids. Now you only hear about it happening once in a blue moon again.'

'What's your point? Are you saying that those kids didn't get attacked?'

'No, nothing like that. I guess what I'm saying is that things like that must happen all the time but no-one's interested. As soon as it makes the news, though, people start to report it and before you know it you've got dogs biting kids on every street corner.'

'Not sure if I agree with you,' she says quietly. 'Still not even sure I know what you're talking about. There's never been anything on this scale before—'

'I think that these idiots,' I explain, pointing at the TV, 'are doing more harm than good. By giving these people a label and giving them airtime they're glorifying whatever it is that's happening and blowing it out of all proportion. People are seeing the violence and the glory and rebellion on TV and they're thinking, I'll have some of that.'

'Bullshit. You're starting to sound like Dad.'

'It's not bullshit. Remember those riots last summer?' I ask, luckily managing to think of another example to try and strengthen my tenuous argument. About eight months ago there was a string of race-motivated disturbances in a few major cities, ours included. Lizzie nods her head.

'What about them?'

'Same thing again. Someone started a little bit of trouble out of the way in some back-street somewhere. The media got hold of it and the problem was made to look a hundred times worse than it ever was. It was the way they reported it that made it spread and maybe that's what's happening now. There's a genuine problem somewhere that gets reported and before you know it you've got mobs in every city starting trouble using whatever it was that caused the very first fight to kick off as an excuse to get involved.'

'And do you really believe that?'

I stay quiet. I don't honestly know what I believe.

'I think you're talking crap,' she snaps. 'None of what you've said explains why I watched a perfectly healthy and normal eleven-year-old boy beat the hell out of the headteacher this morning, does it?'

I still stay quiet. I'm relieved when, at long last, something different happens on the news channel. The usual presenters behind their expensive-looking desk have suddenly disappeared and we're now watching a round table discussion between four people who are probably all politicians or experts in some field or other. They've already been talking for a couple of minutes so we've missed the introductions.

'What are they going to be able to tell us?' I grumble. 'How can these people be experts if no-one knows what's happening yet?'

'Just shut up so we can listen,' Lizzie sighs.

I can't help being sceptical. The whole set-up reminds me of the start of that film *Dawn of the Dead* where the views of another so-called expert are ripped apart by a non-believing TV presenter. I know we're not dealing with a zombie apocalypse here but the way these people are talking to each other makes it feel eerily similar. No-one's backing up what they say with any facts. No-one has anything to offer other than half-baked theories and ideas. No-one seems to believe what anyone else is saying.

'The police force is already operating at full stretch and our hospitals are struggling to cope with the increase in injuries,' a grey-haired lady is saying. 'The situation must be brought under control soon or we will not have the capacity to react. If this situation continues indefinitely, and at the rate of increase we're presently seeing, we'll be in danger of reaching saturation point where we simply will not be able to deal with what's happening.'

'But what *is* happening?' someone finally asks. It's a middle-aged man. I think he's a doctor. Not sure if he's a medic or a shrink. 'Surely our priority must be to identify the cause and resolve that first.'

'I think with this situation the cause *and* the effect are one and the same,' a small, balding man (who, I believe, is a fairly senior politician) says. 'People are reacting to what they see on the streets, and their reactions are making the situation appear far worse than it actually is.'

'See,' I say, nudging Liz.

'Shh . . .' she hisses.

'Do you seriously believe that?' the other man challenges. 'Do you really believe that any of this is happening purely as a result of the violence we've already seen?'

'The violence is a by-product,' the grey-haired lady says.

'The violence is part and parcel of the problem,' the politician argues. 'The violence *is* the problem. Once we've restored order we can start to—'

'The violence is a by-product,' the grey-haired lady says again, annoyed that she's been interrupted. 'You're right in as far as there is a huge element of copycat violence, but the violence is *not* the cause. There's an underlying reason for what's happening which needs to be identified before—'

'There's no evidence to suggest that's the case,' the politician says quickly.

'There's no *published* evidence to suggest that's the case,' the middle-aged man snaps, 'but how much unpublished information is being withheld? This is unprecedented. With an escalation in trouble of this scale there has to be an identifiable cause, doesn't there? For this to be happening independently in so many different geographical regions there has to be an identifiable cause.'

'If you look at what we've seen over the last few days,' the politician says, shaking his head, 'there has been a steady increase in the recorded levels of violence around major cities where there are high population levels. This is wholly expected. With situations like this the more people who are concentrated in a particular geographic area, the more likely it is that trouble will develop there . . .'

I stop listening. I sense that this bureaucrat is launching into some prearranged spiel in which he'll no doubt deny all cover-ups and hidden agendas. This sounds like more bullshit. The other people taking part in the debate challenge him but, although he squirms and struggles to keep control, he ultimately remains tight-lipped. I get the feeling that this programme might have been arranged as a public relations exercise but it's failing miserably. The politician's unease and the way he's blatantly avoiding the questions people are putting to him means one of two things. Either the government knows full well what's happening and is simply choosing not to tell the public, or the authorities genuinely don't have a clue. Both alternatives are equally frightening.

Twenty minutes more of the news channel and my eyes are starting to close. The debate is over and the headlines are back on. They say that the military may be drafted in to help maintain law and order if the police do become over-stretched as the grey-haired panellist suggested in the debate earlier. They also say that the problem is largely limited to major cities and there are, as yet, no reports of it spreading to other countries. Most worryingly of all, there's talk of an after-dark curfew and other restrictions being introduced to keep people off the streets and out of each other's faces.

It's what isn't being said that bothers me. I'm just concerned that no-one seems to have a clue what's going on.

TUESDAY

vi

Jeremy Pearson felt like he was about to be sick. He'd been okay when he'd been prepped for the operation, but now he was actually lying on the table in the operating theatre with people crowding around him and machines beeping and buzzing and that huge round light hanging over him he was beginning to feel nauseous and faint. *I should have gone for the general anaesthetic not a local*, he thought to himself as Dr Panesar the surgeon walked towards him. *I'm paying enough for this operation as it is, a general anaesthetic wouldn't have cost that much more . . .*

'Okay, Mr Pearson,' he said through his green cloth face mask, 'how are you feeling?'

'Not too good,' Pearson mumbled, too afraid to move. He tensed his body underneath the sheet and gown which covered him.

'This won't take too long,' Dr Panesar explained, ignoring his patient's nerves. 'You're the fourth vasectomy I've done today and none of them have lasted much longer than half an hour so far. We'll have you out of here before you know it.'

Pearson didn't respond. He was feeling faint. Maybe it was the heat in the theatre or was it just the thought of what was about to happen that was making him feel like this? Was this normal? Was he having a reaction to the anaesthetic they'd used to numb the feeling in his balls?

'I don't feel . . .' he tried to say to the female nurse who stood next to him, holding onto his arm. She looked down and, seeing that he was struggling, slipped an oxygen mask over his face.

'You'll be fine,' she soothed. 'Have a bit of air and try and think about something else.'

Pearson tried to answer but his words were muffled under the mask. *How can I think about something else when someone's about to cut into my balls?*

'Do you follow cricket?' an older male nurse on his other side asked. Pearson nodded. 'Have you seen the tour report today? We're not doing too badly by all accounts.'

The oxygen was beginning to take the edge off his nausea. That's better. Starting to feel more relaxed now . . .

'Okay, Mr Pearson,' Dr Panesar said brightly, looking up from the area of the operation. 'We're ready to start now. I explained what I'm going to do in clinic, didn't I? This is a very small procedure. I'll just be making two incisions, one on either side of your scrotum, okay?'

Pearson nodded. I don't want to know what you're doing, he thought, just bloody well get on with it.

'You feeling a bit better now?' the female nurse asked, gently stroking the back of his hand. He nodded again and she removed the oxygen mask. He could feel the surgeon working now. Although his genitals were anaesthetised, he could still feel movement around his legs and occasionally someone brushed against the tips of his toes sticking out over the end of the operating table. More nausea. He was starting to feel sick again. Christ, think of something to take your mind off this, he silently screamed to himself. He tried to fill his head with images and thoughts – the children, his wife Emily, the holiday they'd booked for a few weeks' time, the new car he'd picked up last week . . . anything. As hard as he tried he still couldn't forget the fact that someone was cutting into his scrotum with a scalpel.

Is this how I'm supposed to feel? Pearson thought. I'm cold. I don't feel right. Should it be like this or is something going wrong?

'Don't feel right . . .' he mumbled. The nurse looked down and slammed the oxygen mask on his face again. The sudden movement made Dr Panesar look up.

'Everything okay up there?' he asked, his voice artificially bright and animated. 'You all right, Mr Pearson?'

'He's fine,' the nurse replied, her voice equally artificially trouble-free, 'a little light-headed, that's all.'

'Nothing to worry about,' the surgeon said as he took a step around the edge of the table and looked into his patient's face. Pearson's wide, frightened eyes were dancing around the room, squinting into the bright lights which shone down over his prone body. Dr Panesar stopped and stared at him.

'Dr Panesar?' the nurse asked.

Nothing.

'Is everything all right, Dr Panesar?'

Panesar stumbled back to the other end of the table, his eyes still fixed on Pearson's face.

'You okay, Dr Panesar?' his surgical assistant asked. No response. 'Dr Panesar,' he asked again, 'are you okay?'

Panesar turned to look at his colleague and then tightened the grip on the scalpel in his hand. Crouching back down again he slashed across Pearson's exposed genitals and severed his testicles and scrotal sac. Blood began to spill and spurt over the operating table from sliced veins and arteries.

'What the hell are you doing?' the surgical assistant demanded. He pushed Panesar out of the way and moved to grab his hand and wrestle the scalpel from him. Delirious with fear, Panesar turned and sliced the man with the blade, cutting him open in a diagonal line down from his right shoulder.

Panic erupted in the operating theatre. The staff scattered as the surgeon lunged towards them. Pearson lay helplessly on the operating table, turning his head desperately from side to side, trying to see what was happening around him. Covered in blood and still brandishing the scalpel Panesar fled from the room. Pearson watched him run. What the hell was going on? Christ, he suddenly felt strange. He felt cold and shaky but his legs felt warm. And why were people panicking? Why all the sudden movement? Why had the nurses gone to the other end of the table and where was all that blood coming from?

Still anaesthetised and oblivious and ignorant both to the pandemonium which was rapidly spreading through the private hospital and the fact that he was rapidly bleeding to death, Pearson looked up into the light and tried to think of anything but the fact that his surgeon had just disappeared in the middle of his vasectomy.

12

There's a strange atmosphere everywhere today. Everyone seems to be on edge. No-one seems certain about anything any more. Everybody seems to be thinking twice about everything they do and worrying more than normal about what everyone else is doing. Our ordinary lives and the day-to-day routine suddenly feel more complicated than they did before and yet I'm still not even sure if anything's actually changed.

I had a phone call from Lizzie just after I'd been out for my lunch break today. We had an appointment to take Josh for a hospital check-up this afternoon and, with everything that happened at school yesterday, we'd both forgotten about it. He fell off a chair at playgroup three weeks ago and cut his head open. The appointment was just to make sure that everything had healed properly and that he was fit and well. Lizzie had also forgotten to tell Harry that school was closed. He arrived on the doorstep at eight this morning expecting to be looking after Josh as usual. Liz arranged for him to drive her and Josh into town, then take Ellis and Ed back home. I said I'd meet them at the hospital and we'd travel home together after he'd seen the doctor. I managed to convince Tina Murray that I needed to be at the appointment too. For once she bought my story without putting up much of a fight.

Despite trying to make a quick getaway I was later leaving the office than I should have been (I stopped to chat to someone) and it's taken me ages to get across town. Josh's appointment was at three o'clock – three-quarters of an hour ago. Still, hospitals are always behind and with everything that's going on there's bound to be more delays than usual today. I bet he hasn't even gone in to see the doctor yet. I walk quickly down the sloping path which cuts through the car park. The hospital looks busy. The afternoon is dull and dark and bright yellow light shines out from the building's countless windows. It's a bloody grim place. I wouldn't want to have to stay here for . . .

'Danny!'

Who the hell was that? I turn around and see Lizzie walking towards me with Josh in his pushchair.

'You okay?' I ask, confused.

'Where've you been?'

'I couldn't get here any earlier,' I answer, lying through my teeth. 'Have you only just got here?'

She shakes her head.

'You're joking, aren't you? We've already been in.'

'What, he's had his appointment?'

'It was booked for three o'clock. It's a good job you weren't taking him.'

'I know but—'

'We've been waiting for you for the last twenty minutes. We were in and out in seconds. They rushed us through.'

'I'm sorry, I . . .'

She shakes her head again and starts to push Josh up the hill back towards the main road.

'Doesn't matter,' she mumbles. Christ, she's in a bad mood.

'And is everything okay?' I ask, having to shout after her as she storms away. 'Is Josh all right?'

'He's fine,' she grunts back over her shoulder.

The afternoon goes from bad to worse. Lizzie's talking to me again now but she's still not happy. Neither am I. We've walked back across town to the station but there's been a problem with the lines and our train has been cancelled. We can't get Harry to collect us (there isn't enough room in the car) so the only option left is a long journey home on three buses. Liz has just phoned Harry and told him we'll be late back. By all accounts he's not at all impressed.

The working day is drawing to a close. The light is fading and those office workers who finish at four o'clock are already starting to crowd onto the streets. We need to get out of town quickly or we'll get caught up in the main rush-hour crush.

'Which bus?' Lizzie asks, having to shout to make herself heard over the traffic.

'The 220,' I answer from just behind her. I'm pushing Josh now and we seem to be moving in the opposite direction to almost every other pedestrian. It's hard to keep moving forward in a straight line. 'The stop's just up here.'

Our stop is halfway down a one-way street. Lizzie ducks into the shelter and I follow. Josh is moaning. He's cold and hungry.

'Look, I'm sorry I didn't make it to the hospital on time,' I say. 'Things are difficult at the moment. You know what it's like when—'

'Doesn't matter,' she interrupts, obviously not interested in my explanations.

I peer down the street as a bus appears. I hopefully squint into the distance to make out the number but it's not ours. I slump into the shelter again.

'So what did the doctor say?'

'Nothing much. We were in and out in five minutes. His head's healed as it should have and there's no lasting damage. He'll have a small scar but it'll be hidden by his hair.'

'That's good,' I say, looking down at Josh who, somehow, now looks like he's about to fall asleep. 'It's a relief. You can never be sure when they hurt themselves like that . . .'

I stop talking when a sudden stampede of footsteps thunders past the bus stop. A group of six men are chasing after a single shaven-headed figure who is desperately trying to get away. He's wearing jeans and a white T-shirt which is covered in blood. Two of the men barge past us and almost knock Lizzie over.

'Watch where you're going you fucking idiots!' I shout after them. I immediately regret opening my mouth. Lizzie glares at me. Thankfully both of the men keep running and neither of them reacts.

The man they're all chasing sprints into the street and runs immediately into the path of a taxi which blasts its horn and flashes its lights at him. The driver swerves and skids to a halt and some-how manages to avoid a collision. The man pushes himself away off the bonnet of the taxi and turns and starts to run down the middle of the road. But the slight delay is his downfall and the group of men following are onto him like wild animals chasing down their prey. My heart is in my mouth. The rest of the world seems to have stopped still.

The nearest of the chasing pack reaches out and manages to grab hold of the man's sleeve. With a single strong yank he pulls the desperate figure backwards. He trips over his own feet and falls in a crumpled heap on the dotted white line in the middle of the road.

'Fucking scum,' I hear one of the other men shout. 'You fucking Hater scum.'

They encircle the lone runner and batter him. They kick and hit him relentlessly. I look at Lizzie and she stares back at me, her eyes wide with shock and fear. Does she expect me to do something? There's no way I'm getting involved. I look around and see that no-one else is doing anything either. The traffic has ground to a halt and many of the pedestrians on either side of the road have stopped walking.

The beating lasts for less than a minute. They surround him and batter him from every side and every angle, kicking his face, his kidneys, his chest and his bollocks and stamping on his head, his kneecaps and his outstretched hands. Once the frenzied attack is over the man's breathless assailants step back, leaving the twitching body on the ground in full view. The wail of approaching sirens shatters the heavy and ominous silence. I look back down the road and see that a police motorbike is weaving through the stationary traffic. By the time the police officer reaches the body all but one of the attackers have disappeared into the crowds. The one who remains stands his ground and shouts and screams at the officer and points accusingly at the helpless, broken man on the road before turning and running after the others. With a bizarre lack of urgency, interest and care the police officer drags the body away from the middle of the road and leaves it in the gutter before signalling to the traffic to start moving again.

The world slowly starts to crank itself back into action.

Lizzie is holding onto my arm, gripping me so tight that it hurts. I can't take my eyes off the dark mound at the side of the road. Who was it? What had he done? If he really was a Hater then he deserved everything he got.

It seems like every time we go out now something happens.

I think back to the television programme we watched last night, and then I think about the other attacks I've seen and those I've heard about. All that bullshit I came out with last night suddenly seems to count for nothing. There *is* something more to this. This isn't just paranoia or people exploiting the situation.

I feel sick with nerves and fear.

Who is it going to happen to next? Me? Lizzie? Harry or one of the kids? Someone at work? It could be anyone.

13

It's late by the time we finally get home. We'd expected to be back by five. There were more traffic delays on the way out of town. It's now almost eight.

'Someone's in a hurry,' one of the men from the flat upstairs says as we pass him on his way out of the apartment block. I think this is Gary. He has another man with him who I've never seen before.

'Sorry,' I mumble as I struggle to get through the entrance door with Josh's pushchair.

'You all right?' he asks, appearing genuinely concerned.

'We're fine, thanks,' I answer quickly, not interested in talking. I gently push Lizzie towards the flat. The two men leave.

'Everything okay?' Harry asks as I open our front door. He's halfway down the hall as soon as he hears the key in the lock. 'I've been worried sick about you. You could have phoned me again.'

'Sorry, Dad,' Lizzie says.

'There was some trouble,' I explain.

'What kind of trouble?'

Liz takes off her coat and shakes her head. She wipes her eyes.

'I don't know what's going on out there,' she sighs, her voice quiet and emotional. 'It feels like the whole world's going mad.'

'So what happened?' he asks, looking from Lizzie to me and then back again for an answer. 'Are you both all right? Did you . . . ?'

'We're okay,' she says wearily as she gently pushes him back down the corridor towards the living room. Josh is still asleep. I carefully unbuckle his straps, take off his coat and pick him up out of the pushchair.

'What happened?' Harry asks again as I follow him and Liz into the living room. I stop and quickly look into the children's bedrooms. Ed's lying on his bed reading. Ellis's room is empty.

'We walked down to Pedmore Row to catch the bus,' I tell him. 'Group of blokes came out of nowhere and started kicking hell out of this guy. He was a Hater. Where's Ellis?'

Harry nods towards the living room. I peer over the back of the sofa and I'm relieved to see her curled up in a ball asleep with her grandad's jumper draped over her shoulders. She looks peaceful and relaxed. The room is quiet and dark and the only light comes from the flickering TV in the corner.

'She wouldn't go to bed,' he explains, standing and watching her with me. 'Kept asking where you two were. I let her stay with me for a while. I knew she'd fall asleep eventually.'

Liz crouches down in front of Ellis and brushes a strand of hair away from her face.

'I'll take her back to bed,' she whispers as she carefully slides her arms underneath her and lifts her up. Ellis mumbles and shuffles but she doesn't wake up. Harry and I watch as she carries her away. Harry then walks around and sits down in the middle of the sofa where he's probably been sitting all evening. I lay Josh down on my lap.

'So tell me again,' he says quietly, 'what exactly did happen?'

I sit down next to him and kick off my shoes.

'I don't know any more than what I've already told you. A group of blokes lynched a Hater, that's all. Evil bastard probably deserved everything he got. Then the bus was late and a road was closed and . . .'

Harry nods his head, sighs and rubs his eyes. He looks tired.

'I don't know what's going on out there,' he says quietly. 'Anyway, I'm glad you're back. I had a feeling you might have some trouble tonight.' I'm about to ask him what he means when he grabs the remote control and turns up the volume on the TV. 'Been watching the news since the children's programmes finished,' he explained. 'Things are getting out of control.'

I turn my attention from Harry to the TV. There's been no let-up in the level of trouble across the country. On the news they're talking about an 'exponential increase in incidents'. Mathematics was never my strongest subject at school but I know what they mean. One incident becomes two, two becomes four, four becomes eight and it goes on and on until . . . Jesus, where's this going to end?

There's a definite change in the way the reporters on TV are talking about what's happening tonight. They're concentrating on the people – the so-called Haters – who seem to be at the root of all the troubles. They're stressing that it's only a very small minority who have been affected but they're warning the public to stay away from anyone who appears to be behaving erratically. Bloody hell, that's half the population of this town on a good day.

'It's like a disease,' Harry says. 'Crazy, isn't it? It's spreading just like a disease.'

'Someone better hurry up and find a cure then,' I mutter under my breath, still staring at the screen.

'They keep saying that all of this is down to just a few people, you know,' he continues, repeating what I've already heard. 'When it gets them, whatever it is, it drives them mad. They had some doctor on talking about it earlier. It's the first few minutes you have to watch out for.'

'What?' I mumble, only half listening.

'When it gets them they lose control, like that chap you saw tonight I expect. They just lash out at whoever or whatever's around them. Then they say they start to calm down. They're still capable of doing these things, but they're not quite so volatile.'

What is he talking about?

'What do you mean, not quite so volatile?' I ask him. 'Are you saying they'll only do enough to hospitalise you and not kill you?'

'I'm only telling you what I've heard,' he sighs. 'I won't bother if you're going to be like that.'

I shake my head and look back at the TV. The screen is filled with images of convoys of troops driving into a city centre somewhere. Not sure where it is but it's nowhere I recognise. The reporters are talking about the police and armed forces being used to full capacity and I think back to the TV debate we watched last night. Have we reached the saturation point they were talking about yet? The voices on the TV are taking great pains to stress that, although stretched, the authorities are still coping. Just. Christ, imagine what will happen if this thing gets any bigger and they can't cope. Bloody hell, it doesn't bear thinking about.

The screen shows a stream of government statistics and I lose interest. I don't believe statistics. They're all made up. They can make statistics say whatever they want.

'Problem is,' Harry says, 'they've let it get out of control. This is too little, too late.'

'It?' I say. 'What's "it" supposed to be?'

He points at the screen.

'The trouble,' he answers, 'the violence . . . the people.'

The statistics have gone and we're left watching footage of a row of burning houses. Desperate, screaming people are being held back by a police blockade. All they can do is watch as their lives go up in flames.

'What's happening,' he whispers secretively, 'is people are panicking and overreacting to the slightest thing because of what they're seeing and what they're being told. The whole situation has been allowed to get out of proportion. People are seeing the death and the destruction on the television and it's making them want to become a part of it too. It's like those bloody awful horror films that you and Lizzie watch. They make you want to do things. They put ideas in your head and they make you think it's all right to do things. They're even giving these people a label now. Calling them "Haters" for God's sake. They're glamorising it. Almost makes it sound like a club you'd want to join, doesn't it?'

He's saying the same kind of things I was saying just yesterday. But I've already begun to accept that I was wrong, and when I look at the TV screen tonight I'm even more sure that I'd misjudged the situation badly when I was rambling last night. The sheer scale of what's happening is really beginning to scare me now. They keep talking about small minorities but thousands, possibly even tens of sands, of people are involved in this violence. Hundreds of lives are affected by every incident in some way. Young, old, male, female . . . people from every section of society are involved. This is far more than just paranoia. This is more than the media stirring things up.

'I don't want to join any club,' I tell him, 'and no-one's put any ideas in my head. I haven't started any fights. I'm no more going to go out and attack anyone than you or Lizzie are.'

'I know that. We've got maturity and common sense on our side though, haven't we? We know the difference between right and wrong. We know what's acceptable and what isn't.'

'Are you trying to say that everyone who's been affected by this is just immature? Come on, Harry, do you really think—'

'There are plenty of people out there who couldn't give a damn about right or wrong,' he continues, ignoring me. 'There are people who get a kick out of causing trouble, and putting it on the television like this has just made things worse. By showing it they're saying it's all right, that it's acceptable.'

'Bullshit! They're not saying that at all—'

'They're implying that because so many people are involved now, anyone left might as well join in.'

'Bullshit!' I say again.

'There's no need to swear at me,' he snaps.

'You're so wrong,' I try to explain. 'It's got nothing to do with—'

'And that's just the kind of thing I'm talking about,' he continues, raising his voice and still not listening to any of what I'm trying to say. 'Thirty years ago you'd never have used that kind of language in everyday conversation. Now every other word you hear is a curse. Standards have slipped and that is what's happening out there on the streets.'

For a moment I can't answer. The old man has suddenly become very agitated. His face is flushed red with anger and a terrifying thought flashes into my mind. Is he a Hater? Is he about to change? Is he going to become like those people we've seen on TV? Is he about to attack me? Should I attack him first before he has chance to get me? Is this how it begins . . . ?

'No-one has any respect for anything or anyone else any more,' he continues. 'It's a bloody disgrace. It's been coming for years. Before you know it we'll have total anarchy and you'll see—'

'I know what you're trying to say, Dad,' Lizzie interrupts, returning to the room, 'but I don't agree. Danny and I had this conversation last night, didn't we? I've never seen anything like the things I've seen over the last few days. I've seen plenty of trouble before, but never anything like this.'

I relax. Liz's sudden arrival seems to have calmed the situation. The anger in Harry's face has gone.

'What do you mean? What's different?' he asks. Liz stands in the doorway and thinks for a few seconds.

'Out there tonight, after they'd beaten that man, you could almost taste it in the air.'

'Taste what?' I wonder.

'The fear,' she replies. 'People are scared. People are already starting to expect trouble and they're tensing up ready for it. And when it happens they react, most of the time completely out of character from what I've seen. I don't know what's causing any of this, Dad, but I do know there has to be a definite, physical reason for it. People are bloody frightened and the situation's getting worse by the day.'

'Things will start to calm down . . .' Harry starts to say instinctively. Lizzie's shaking her head.

'No, they won't,' she says, her voice trembling and unsteady. 'We watched a group of men lynch a Hater tonight. I don't know what he'd done, but it couldn't have been any worse than the way they retaliated. There was as much hate and anger coming from them as anyone else.'

WEDNESDAY

vii

Daryl Evans sat at the back of the top floor of the bus as it wound its way through the streets towards the city centre. He leant against the window and looked down as he headed towards the council offices where he worked and yet another day of grind and grief. He didn't feel like working today. Maybe he'd try and leave after a couple of hours, he thought. Maybe he'd tell Tina, his supervisor, that he didn't feel well and that he needed to go home. With everything that was happening right now he didn't think she'd try stopping him.

Evans wasn't particularly interested in the rest of the world. He didn't pay much attention to anything that happened outside his immediate circle of family and friends. He'd had a good night last night and that made it harder to motivate himself this morning. He'd spent some time with a friend he hadn't seen for a while. They'd spent the evening drinking beer and eating junk food. He still felt bloated and a little hung-over this morning. He'd slept through his alarm and then turned the flat upside down looking for his watch. He'd eventually found it under his bed but by then he was already late leaving for work. He just knew it was going to be one of those days where everything takes more effort than it should and nothing goes right.

Evans didn't have any time for news and current affairs. He didn't know why the streets were quiet this morning or why he'd had to wait twice as long as usual for a bus which was half-empty. He did notice that things felt different today, but he really couldn't be bothered to try and work out why.

There were seven other people on the top floor of the bus. Five of them sat alone, quiet and thoughtful, watching the grey and damp morning outside. A couple sat together towards the front, laughing and joking with each other and making more noise than the rest of the passengers combined. Evans sat right at the back and watched them all. The inside of the bus was steaming up with condensation.

He wiped the window clean so that he could see how far he'd got left to travel. His sudden movement caught the attention of a pencil-thin, wiry-haired man sitting two rows of seats ahead who nervously turned round to see what was happening behind him.

Evans made eye contact with the other passenger and froze.

The man – quiet, unassuming and not wanting any trouble – quickly turned back and faced the front of the bus again, praying that nothing was going to happen. It was too late. Evans, filled with a sudden uncontrollable fear and compulsion, jumped up and pulled the other passenger out of his seat. He shoved him down into the aisle between the two rows of seats and he landed with a heavy thump which was loud enough to be heard by everyone on the lower floor. He looked down at the man, who stared back up at him petrified, his shoulders wedged between the seats on either side. Evans raised his foot and stamped on his face, breaking his nose and splitting the skin under his right eye. Then he stamped again, then again and again, feeling any resistance almost immediately fade and then feeling the man's bones beginning to crack beneath the force of his relentless attack.

The driver looked up in her monitor but the rush of top floor passengers getting up from their seats and running down the steep staircase blocked her view. She brought her bus to a sudden halt in the middle of a usually busy dual carriageway. A week ago many people would have tried to do something to help, but not today. Terrified and fearing for their own safety they ran as quickly as they could, spilling out onto the street and looking up at the occasional flashes of movement they could see from the bloody and violent attack which continued on the top floor.

Two police officers who had been patrolling nearby were inside the bus before the last passengers had scrambled out. They climbed the stairs at speed, batons raised and ready. Daryl Evans threw himself at them. A single well-aimed smash of a truncheon across the side of his head knocked him out cold and he collapsed to the ground, falling just inches away from the lifeless feet of the body of the man he'd just beaten to death.

14

Lizzie called me a bloody idiot for coming here today. She said I was mad going into town and now I'm here I have to agree. I wanted to stay at home but I had no choice. I've had too much time off recently. I was disciplined because of my absence record a couple of months back and now I don't get paid if I don't go in. They've threatened to kick me out if I don't turn up for work, and no matter how much I hate this job I can't afford to lose it. Maybe I'll be the only one who turns up today. Maybe I should just take a chance and turn round and go back home anyway. I don't know what's worse – the thought of sitting through another disciplinary meeting with Barry Penny and Tina or risking getting caught up in the kind of trouble we saw here last night.

The streets are quieter today. There are still plenty of people around but it feels more like a Sunday morning than a Wednesday. Everyone is silent and subdued and hardly anyone is talking to anyone else. I understand why it's like this. I don't want to talk to anyone either. I don't want to risk making any contact – even just looking at them – if there's a chance trouble's going to flare up. I keep my head down and my mouth shut and I guess that's what everyone else is doing too.

This feels bizarre. Last night when we were coming home from the hospital and later when I was talking to Harry it began to feel like the world was falling apart and coming to an end. The reality this morning feels different. Despite the quiet and the lack of conversation everything appears outwardly normal. It's hard to believe the things we've seen and heard about.

I cross Millennium Square to get to the office. It's a huge expanse of block-paving with a horrible modern fountain stuck right in the middle of it. It's right in the centre of town and people cross it from all directions to get to wherever it is they're supposed to be going. It's always busy. Between eight o'clock and nine in the morning, midday and two in the afternoon and pretty much anytime after four o'clock right through to the early hours this place is choc full of people. If there's a place you'd expect something to happen, this is it. Maybe I should have avoided it today, but that would have added at least another ten minutes to my walk to work and I'm running late as it is. It looks as if the authorities are ready for trouble. There are more police officers patrolling around here than I've ever seen on duty before and most, if not all of them, are armed. That might be normal elsewhere in the world but not here. Jesus, seeing officers walking through the crowd with their semi-automatic weapons primed and ready to fire makes me realise just how dangerous and unpredictable the situation now is. But surely their presence will just add to the problem, not diffuse it?

My last couple of minutes of freedom before I reach the office.

What is causing this to happen? As I walk through the silent, stony-faced crowds I can't help but wonder again what's responsible for all this madness and hysteria. What is it that's turning the world on its head? Has this whole situation been manufactured by the media as Lizzie's dad believes or is there more to it? Has anything really happened at all? Are people running scared from something that doesn't even exist? Or is there something in the water? Has something been sprayed into the air by terrorists? Are we living through some bizarre *Invasion of the Body Snatchers* type scenario?

Or is it something worse than all of that?

Midday.

Less than half of the staff turned up for work today. I've tried to keep my head down as much as I can. Keeping busy makes the time go faster and I want today to pass as quickly as possible. I briefly spoke to Liz an hour or so ago. The school is closed again. They tried to open this morning but only half the children turned up and even fewer staff so Lizzie is spending another day stuck at home with the kids. They're driving her crazy but I know she's happier there. Wish I was back there too.

The lack of staff today means we're all stretched. Jennifer Reynolds is one of the people who hasn't turned up and that's meant all of us taking turns to cover Reception in hour-long shifts. If ever there was a day I didn't want to be out there it's today. Even Tina's had to take a turn. I've just finished my shift and Hilary

Turner has come out to relieve me. I like Hilary. She's a sour-faced, frosty old spinster who's grossly overweight but she knows who does what around here and she doesn't take any crap. Unlike most of the other people I work with she's straight and honest. If she's got a problem with something you've done then she'll tell you to your face – none of the backstabbing bullshit you get from everyone else. She's hard as nails and I like her all the better for it.

'It's been quiet,' I tell her as she waddles towards me. 'No-one's been in.'

'That's the kiss of death,' she grumbles as she slumps heavily into the hot seat behind the desk, 'they'll all start dragging themselves in here now I've come out.'

I'm about to tell her to shut up and stop being stupid when the main door flies open. She might be right. There's a sudden flurry of movement as a man storms into the building. He's carrying a handful of papers which he slams down onto the desk in front of Hilary. She jumps back. This guy is furious. He's seething with anger and suddenly I'm too scared to move. Is he one of them? Is he a Hater?

'Sort this out,' he screams. 'Sort this bloody mess out now!'

He slams his fist down on the counter again. His face is flushed red and he's breathing heavily. He's over six foot tall and he's built like a bloody rugby player. I should say something to him but I can't. I'm silently willing Hilary to speak (she's usually good at dealing with this sort of thing) but she's struck dumb too.

'You fucking people have clamped my car,' he yells. 'There were no signs and no markings. This is an absolute fucking disgrace. I've missed a meeting because of you people . . .'

I still can't move. He's still shouting but I've stopped listening to what he's saying. I stare into his face and slowly shuffle further back until I'm pressed up against the wall. Is this man really a Hater? Oh Christ, is he about to explode and kill us both? What the hell do I do? Do I just run? The man looks at Hilary and then at me. I try not to make eye contact but I can't help it. I can see Hilary out of the corner of my eye. She's shaking like a leaf. She's usually rock hard but she's as frightened as I am. I have to do something.

'Look . . .' I start to say, my voice quiet and unsteady.

'Don't give me any bullshit,' he snaps, his voice no quieter or calmer, 'I don't want any bullshit. Just get this sorted out and do it now. I need to get back to my office. I'm at the end of my fucking tether here and if I don't get . . .'

He leans forward again and we both physically recoil.

'Please . . .' Hilary mumbles meekly. She starts to sob. Under the desk she presses the personal attack alarm. I can hear the high-pitched screech of the alert ringing out in the main office.

The man stops. His expression changes. He hears the sound too. He looks from me to Hilary and back again once more. His eyes are suddenly wide with shock and panic. What the hell's he got to be afraid of? He's the one who came in here and . . .

'I'm sorry,' he says quickly, taking a couple of steps back away from the desk. 'I'm sorry, I didn't mean to . . .'

Realisation dawns.

His voice is now at a fraction of its previous volume. Hilary and I are stood there, just waiting for him to explode again. Instead he crumbles. He realises that we're scared and now he's the one who's frightened that we're going to react.

'I'm not one of them,' he says, pleading with us to believe him. He looks like he has tears in his eyes. 'Honest I'm not. The parking ticket made me mad and I just over reacted, that's all. I'm not a Hater. I don't want to fight. I'm not going to hurt anyone . . .'

I still can't do anything. I'm frozen to the spot. This whole situation feels alien and bizarre. It's an uneasy standoff which ends as quickly as it began. The man seems to be about to say something else but he doesn't. Instead he turns and walks out of the building, still clutching his parking ticket.

15

Lunchtime. It's a couple of hours later than I'd originally planned to take my break. It would have been more sensible and probably safer to stay in the office but I've had to come outside. I had another call from Lizzie. Her day trapped at home with the kids is getting worse. We need bread and milk but they're acting up and she can't face taking them anywhere. I said I'd get some while I was here. I was going to wait until after work but I'm glad I didn't. The supermarket shelves were almost empty. There won't be anything left tonight.

Without thinking I find myself back in Millennium Square again. It's still not as busy as it normally is but there are plenty of people here and . . .

What the hell was that?

I'm stood in the middle of the square by the fountain and everything has just gone crazy. Everyone drops to the ground and I do the same. There was a noise – a single loud crack like a gunshot. But it couldn't have been, could it? I slowly lift my head from the ground. People are starting to get up. Some are already running in all directions and it's impossible to see what's happened. Others like me remain unmoving, trying to work out what's going on and where the danger is. I have to move. I have to get out of here. I get up and start to run back in the direction of the office but it's difficult to get through with so many people suddenly zig-zagging all around me. I stop and crouch when I hear the sound again. It *was* a gunshot. It can't have been anything else.

Just to my left a group of people are screaming and yelling in panic. On the ground, right in the middle of them, is a body. I'm not close enough to see any detail but I can see that there's a quickly spreading puddle of blood around the top of the person's head. People start to move again, tripping and stepping over the corpse. Maybe that's it. Maybe it's over now. Maybe that's the body of the Hater lying dead on the ground and things will start to . . .

What now? People are running past me. Have they seen something that I haven't? I've got to get out of here before I get myself . . . too late – there's a third gunshot which comes from my left and which sends the crowd scattering in the opposite direction like frightened pigeons. I have to keep moving but my legs feel as heavy as lead. I'm disorientated. I look up at the buildings around the edges of the square, trying to get my bearings and work out which way to run. When I think I finally know which way to go I take a few quick steps forward, weave around another few frightened people, and then stop dead in my tracks.

The crowd has cleared ahead of me. No more than ten metres in front of me now stands a police officer, armed like those I saw here this morning. He's scanning the square, moving his head slowly from side to side. Now he's stopped and he's lifting his rifle again. Fuck, he's pointing it in my direction. Fucking hell, he's aiming at me! I look straight into his face and he stares back into mine. Do I drop to the ground again? Do I turn and run or . . . ?

Fourth gunshot.

The officer fires and, Jesus Christ, I can almost feel the shot whistle past the side of my face. I slowly look over my shoulder and see another body on the ground not far behind me, a bloody gaping hole in its face where its cheekbone used to be. Shaking, I turn and run. I'm going in the opposite direction from where I want to go but it doesn't matter. I just have to get out of here. What if it's me next? What if he's aiming for me now? Any second and I could hear the crack of the next shot and I could be down with a bullet in my back. I don't have a fucking chance. Just got to keep moving and hope that someone else gets between me and the gunman. Move faster. Move faster I keep telling myself. Keep running. Get yourself out of range. Keep going until . . .

Fifth shot.

Nothing. Didn't hit me.

Sixth, seventh and eighth shots in quick succession. They sounded like they came from a different direction this time? I glance back into the middle of the square.

The armed police officer is down. Another officer stands over him and unloads shots nine, ten and eleven into the twitching body of their former colleague.

I keep running. As I move a single devastating thought crosses my mind. Was that police officer a Hater? Christ, if there are people in the police force who are capable of this kind of cold-blooded, emotionless violence then what the hell are we supposed to do? The implications are vast and terrifying. Who's going to keep control? What the hell happens now?

I have to get home. Fuck work. Forget about the job. I change direction and run as fast as I can towards the station. I have to get back to Lizzie and the kids.

16

Thank God the trains are running today. It took hours to get home yesterday and I don't want to be out on the streets any longer than I have to be tonight. It only took a few minutes to get from the square to the station and I didn't have to wait long for a train. Christ knows what Tina's going to say to me tomorrow if I go back to work. I could call her from my mobile now and explain what's happened but I don't want to. I don't want to speak to anyone. I just want to get home.

There are just three carriages on this train. There can't be any more than twenty people on board. I've found myself a seat as far away from everyone else as possible. This is literally the last seat on the train, right at the very back of the third carriage. There are two other people in here with me. They're both nearer the front, one on either side of the aisle. I find myself trying to watch them constantly, scared that one of them might turn because as long as the train is moving I'm trapped in here with them. Now and then I see one of them look around. They're as anxious as I am. My stomach is churning and I feel like I'm going to throw up. I don't know whether it's the movement of the train or nerves that's making me feel sick.

We're pulling into the last station before home. Christ, I hope no-one gets on here. I've got my mobile phone in my hand and I have had since I got on. I want to call Lizzie and tell her I'm on my way back but I can't bring myself to do it. How stupid is that? I don't want to talk out loud because I don't want to attract any attention to myself. I don't want to do anything that's going to give the other passengers any reason to even look at me.

The train slows down and stops. I look out onto the platform (trying not to make it obvious that I'm staring) and watch as a handful of people shuffle quietly towards the train doors. One person from this carriage gets up and gets off and another passenger arrives. It's a man in a long grey trench coat with a laptop bag slung over his shoulder. I do everything I can to avoid making eye contact with him but I have to keep watching. I have to see where he's going. Is he coming this way? Shit, he is. I quickly look down at the floor now, desperate not to let him know that I was watching. Is he still coming towards me? Is he getting closer?

He's stopped. I'm sure he must have stopped and I can't believe how relieved I suddenly feel. Christ, this is stupid. Am I paranoid? Am I the only one acting this way? I can't believe I am. Very, very carefully and moving very, very slowly I allow myself to look up and around again. The train judders and jolts as it shunts out of the station and I cautiously pull myself up using the back of the seat in front of me for support. The newly arrived passenger is sitting halfway down the carriage on the other side of the aisle. He looks like he's deliberately put as much distance between me and the third passenger as he can. Thank God.

I press my head against the window and watch the familiar sights and landmarks rush by. It all looks the same but everything feels different this afternoon.

Not far now. Almost home.

17

No more bullshit. It's just gone nine and the kids are finally in bed. Now we can drop the pretence. Now we can forget the happy voices and the smiles and laughs we've put on just for their sake. Now Liz and I can sit down together and try and get our heads around what's going on here. There's no point involving the children in any of this. What good would it do? If we can't work it out, what chance have they got? Better that they remain ignorant and happy. Ed's starting to suspect something's wrong but the little two are blissfully unaware. I wish I was.

We've been sat watching the headlines go round on a loop for about twenty minutes.

'This is different tonight,' she says. 'It's changed.'

'What's changed?'

'The news. They've stopped telling us what's happened. You keep watching and you'll see what I mean. All they're doing now is trying to tell us how to deal with things.'

She's right. There's been a definite shift in the focus of the TV news channel we're watching tonight and I hadn't picked up on it until Liz pointed it out. Until now there's been a steady stream of reports about individual attacks and major incidents but all of that has now stopped. Now all that's been broadcast is little more than a series of instructions. They're not telling us anything we haven't already heard – stay away from people you don't know, stay at home if possible, watch out for erratic and irrational behaviour and alert the authorities if trouble breaks out, that sort of thing. It's all straightforward, common-sense stuff.

'Probably not worth wasting time reporting on everything that's happening,' she says. 'One fight in the street's pretty much the same as the next.'

'I know,' I agree. 'There's still something else missing though, isn't there?'

'Like what?'

'If you listen to what they're saying, they're still telling us that everything's under control and the problem's contained but . . .'

'But what?'

'But no-one's coming up with any explanations. No-one's even making any attempt to explain what's happening. That tells me they're either keeping something from us or . . .'

'No-one's managed to work it out yet,' she interrupts before I've had chance to finish my sentence.

18

It's dark. The house is silent. I'm tired but I can't sleep. It's almost two in the morning.

'You awake?' I ask quietly.

'Wide awake,' Lizzie answers.

I roll over onto my side and gently put my arm around her. She does the same and I pull her closer. It feels good to have her next to me like this. It's been too long.

'What are you going to do in the morning?' she asks. The side of her face is touching mine. I can feel her breath on my skin.

'Don't know,' I answer quickly. I want to stay at home but there's a part of me that still thinks I should go back to work. The longer I've lain here awake, the more I've slowly managed to convince myself that it will be safe to go back to the office tomorrow. Stupid bloody idiot. I watched people being shot in the middle of town today. There's no way I can go back there.

'Stay here,' she says quietly. 'Stay here with us. You should be here with me and the children.'

'I know, but . . .' I start to mumble.

'But nothing. We need you here. I need you here. I'm scared.'

I know she's right. I wrap my arms further around her and run my hand down the ridge of her spine. She's wearing a short nightdress. I put my hand underneath it and feel her back again. Her skin is soft and warm. I expect her to grumble and pull away from me like she usually does but she stays where she is. I can feel her hands on my skin now.

'Stay here with me,' she whispers again, slowly moving her hand across my backside and down before sliding it between my legs. She starts to stroke me and despite all the fear, confusion and uncertainty we're both feeling I'm hard in seconds. I can't remember the last time we were intimate. There always seems to be a reason why we can't be close. Something or someone always gets in the way.

'How long's it been?' I ask, keeping my voice low.

'Too long,' she answers.

Lizzie rolls over onto her back and I climb on top of her. I carefully slide inside her and she grips me tightly. I can feel her nails digging into my skin. She wants me as much as I want her. We both need each other tonight. Neither of us says a word. No talking. There's nothing to say.

It's four-thirty. I don't remember what happened. I must have fallen asleep. It's still dark in here and the bed's empty. I look round and see Lizzie standing by the door.

'What's wrong?'

'Listen,' she whispers.

I rub sleep from my eyes and sit up. I can hear noises coming from above us. The sounds are quiet and muffled. Something's happening in the other occupied flat upstairs. There are voices – raised voices – and then the sound of breaking glass.

'What's going on?' I ask, still drugged with sleep.

'This started about five minutes ago,' she explains as the voices above us get louder. 'I couldn't sleep. I thought . . .'

A sudden thump from the flat above interrupts her. Now the whole building is silent. It's a long, uncomfortable and ominous silence which makes me catch my breath. The bedroom is cold and I start to shiver through a combination of the low temperature and nerves. Lizzie turns round to face me and is about to speak when another noise makes her stop. It's the sound of a door slamming upstairs. Seconds later and we hear hurried, uneven footsteps in the lobby outside, then the familiar creak of the front entrance door being pulled open. I start to get out of bed.

'Where are you going?' she asks.

'I just want to see . . .' I start to say although I'm not really sure what I'm doing.

'Don't,' she pleads, 'please don't. Just stay here. Our door's locked and the windows are shut. We're both safe and so are the kids. It doesn't matter about anybody else. Don't get involved. Whatever's going on out there, don't get involved . . .'

I have no intention of going outside, I just want to see what's happening. I go into the living room. I hear a car's engine start and I peer through the curtains, making sure I can't be seen. One of the men from upstairs – I can't see which one – drives away at an incredible speed. I couldn't make out much detail, but I did see that there was only one person in the car and that immediately starts me thinking about who, or what, is left upstairs. I turn around and see that Lizzie is in the living room with me now.

'Maybe I should go up and check . . . ?'

'You're not going anywhere,' she hisses. 'Like I said, our door's locked and the windows are shut. We're safe here and you're not going anywhere.'

'But what if something's happened up there? What if someone's hurt?'

'Then that's someone else's problem. I don't care. All we need to think about is the children and each other. You're not going anywhere.'

I know she's right. Out of duty I pick up the telephone and try to dial the emergency services. Christ, I can't even get an answer.

Lizzie goes back to bed. I'll follow her in a couple of minutes but I already know I won't sleep again tonight. I'm scared. I'm scared because whatever it is that we've seen happening to the rest of the world now suddenly feels a whole lot closer.

THURSDAY

19

I wake up before the alarm goes off and lie still and stare up at the ceiling as I try again to make sense of everything that's happened over the last few days. It all seems implausible and impossible. Has anything actually happened at all? I still can't help wondering if this is all just the result of people's fucked-up and over-enthusiastic imaginations or whether there really is something more sinister and bizarre going on? In the cold light of morning it's difficult to try and comprehend all that I've seen and heard. I start trying to convince myself to get a grip, get up and get ready for work. But then I remember what I saw in Millennium Square yesterday and I'm overcome with nerves and uncertainty as the reality of it all hits me again.

There's no point just lying here. Lizzie and the kids are asleep. It's still dark outside but I get up and shuffle through to the living room. I peer out of the window. The car belonging to the people upstairs still hasn't returned. What happened up there? My mind starts to wander and play tricks. Was there a Hater upstairs? It scares me to think that my kids could have been so close to one of them. I force myself to remember Lizzie's words when we were awake earlier. I have to ignore what's going on everywhere else and concentrate on keeping the people on this side of the front door safe.

The flat feels colder than ever this morning and the low temperature makes me feel old beyond my years. I fetch some breakfast and then sit in front of the TV. I watch cartoons. I can't cope with anything more serious. Not yet.

I'm halfway through a bowl of dry cereal and I can't eat any more. I don't have much of an appetite. I feel uneasy all the time and I can't stop thinking about what's happening out there. What the hell *is* going on? I think about all the unconnected events I've witnessed and the hundreds – probably thousands – of other incidents that have happened elsewhere. No-one can see any connection and yet how can all of these things not be connected? That, I decide, is the most frightening aspect of all. How can so many people from so many different walks of life begin to behave so irrationally and erratically in such a short period of time?

I look over at the clock and realise that I should be getting ready for work now. My stomach starts to turn somersaults when I think about having to phone in and speak to Tina. Christ knows what she's going to say or what I'm going to tell her. Maybe I just won't phone at all.

My curiosity and apprehension gets the better of me. I finally relent and switch on the news. Half of me wants to know what's happening today, the other half wants to go back to bed, put my head under the pillow and not get up again until it's all over. And that causes me to ask myself yet another unanswerable question – how will this end? Will this wave of violence and destruction just fade and die out, or will it keep building and building?

The TV news channel looks different this morning, and for a while I can't put my finger on why. The set is the same and the female presenter is familiar. I don't recognise the man who's sitting next to her. Must be a stand-in. I guess the usual newsreader didn't turn up for work today. Half the staff didn't turn up at my office yesterday. There's no reason why things should be any different for the people on TV, is there? Except, perhaps, the fact that they get paid a hell of a lot more than me for doing a hell of a lot less.

The news is running on a loop again. It seems to be just the headlines on repeat, introduced by these two presenters. There's no sport or entertainment or business news any more, and the reports I'm watching are all similar to those we've seen before. No explanations, just basic information. Occasionally the cycle is interrupted when one of the newsreaders interviews someone in authority. I've seen politicians, religious leaders and others being interviewed over the last few days. They can all talk the talk and most of them know how to play up to the camera, but none of them can disguise the fact that they seem to know as little about what's happening as the rest of us. And there are other people who I would have expected to see interviewed who have been con-spicuous by their absence. What about the Prime Minister and other top-level politicians? Why aren't they showing their faces? Are they too busy personally trying to deal with the crisis (I doubt it) or could it be that they're no longer in office? Could the head of government or the chief of police be Haters?

The male newsreader is talking about schools and businesses remaining closed when a sudden flurry of movement in front of the camera interrupts him. He looks up as a scruffy figure carrying a clipboard and wearing headphones stumbles into view. It's a tall, willowy woman who walks back until she's almost standing right against the newsreaders' desk. Is she a producer or director or something like that? She crouches down slightly to make sure the camera is properly focused on her.

'Don't listen to any more of this rubbish,' she says, her weary face desperate and tear-streaked. 'You're only being told half the story. Don't listen to anything they tell you . . .'

And then she's gone. There's more movement all around her before the pictures disappear and the screen goes black. After a wait of a few more long and uncomfortable seconds the broadcast returns. It's a report about personal safety and security that I've seen at least five times before.

What is it that we're not being told? That woman looked desperate, like she'd been trying to get an opportunity to speak out for days.

I phoned the office a few minutes ago but there was no answer. I was relieved when I didn't have to speak to anyone but then I started to panic again when I thought about how bad things must have got if no-one's turned up for work.

There's nothing else to do now except sit back on the sofa in front of the TV and watch the world fall apart.

20

We need food. The last thing I wanted to do was go outside again but I didn't have any choice. The kids and Lizzie have been trapped at home for the last couple of days and the cupboards are almost empty. We should have thought of it sooner. I need to get some supplies before things get any more uncertain out there.

I have as much cash as I could find in my pocket and I'll see what it will get me. I've always been bad with money. I don't have any credit since I got into a mess with my bank a year or so ago and they cancelled everything on my account. I've got a 'last chance' loan now. Once the payment's gone out on pay day and I've paid the bills I cash the balance and that's what we live on until the next time I get paid. It's two weeks until pay day so I haven't got much left.

I didn't think about where I was going to go until I'd left the flat. Instinctively I drove towards the supermarket we usually use for our weekly shop but I turned back before I got there. Even though it was early there was already a huge queue just to get into the car park. It's a bad-tempered and busy place at the best of times and setting foot in there today would have just been asking for trouble. Two cars collided in the queue just ahead of me. Someone shunted into the back of someone else. Both drivers got out and started screaming and shouting at each other and I got the feeling that the trouble was about to spread. I didn't want to take any chances. I turned around and drove back towards home along roads which were surprisingly quiet. There's still a fair amount of traffic about, but nothing like the number of vehicles you usually get at this time of day.

I'm outside O'Shea's convenience store now. It's only a couple of minutes away from the flat. It's tucked away in a side-street just off the main Rushall Road. It gets most of its trade from the workers at a steel factory just around the corner. It stands to reason that if people aren't going to work today the factory will be closed and the convenience store should be empty. They have a fraction of the stock of the supermarket and they charge double the prices but I don't have any choice. My family needs food and I have to get it from somewhere. I park up (further away than usual) and cross the street.

Bloody hell, as I get nearer to the shop I start to think about turning back again. The building looks like it's in the process of being looted. It's rammed with people and the floor is covered in litter and debris. I force myself to go inside, reminding myself that my family have to eat. Half the displays and freezers are already empty and there's more rubbish and packaging left on the shelves than food. I grab a cardboard box (it's the biggest thing I can find) and start getting what I can. Looks like everyone's had the same idea as me today and they're out panic-buying. I take whatever I can find – cans and packets of food, bottles of sauce, crisps, sweets, spreads – pretty much anything that's salvageable and edible. There's nothing fresh here, no milk or bread or fruit or vegetables.

The shop is small and the mood inside the hot and congested little building is tense. Shopping always seems to bring out the very worst in people. Today I can taste the animosity and nerves in the air but no-one's reacting. Everybody keeps their head down and gets on with stripping the shelves. No-one speaks. No-one makes any intentional contact with anyone else whatsoever. An old guy accidentally elbows me in the ribs as we're both reaching up for the same thing. Normally I'd have had a go at him and he'd probably have had a go back at me. We look at each other for the briefest of moments and then silently take what we can. I don't dare start an argument.

The box is soon two-thirds full with junk. I turn the corner into the last aisle and see two empty check-outs ahead of me. People are just walking past them and there's no sign, unsurprisingly, of any staff. Naively I expected the people I've seen leaving the shop to have paid for the food they were carrying. Should I just take what I've collected? In spite of everything that's happening around me I still feel uneasy at the prospect of walking out with this stuff without paying for it. But I have to do what I have to do. Sod the consequences, I have to think about my family and forget everyone else. This is absolutely crazy. This is looting with manners. Fucking bizarre. I keep loading up the box and edging towards the exit.

There's a scream. Christ, it's a bloody horrible sound and it cuts right through me. People stop moving and look around for the source of the noise. I can see a woman on the ground just behind me. She's lying in the middle of the aisle covering her face with her hands. I try not to stare but I can't help myself. Someone shuffles out of the way and I can see that there's a child attacking her. A girl of maybe eight or nine, no older, is virtually sitting on top of her, punching her and pulling her hair. Jesus, in one hand she's got a tin of food and she's using it to batter the woman. She lands the tin on her forehead and it immediately swells up in a bloody red welt. The woman is screaming and crying and . . . and bloody hell, she's shouting out the girl's name. Is she being beaten by her own daughter? For a fraction of a second I think that I should help her but I know that I can't. None of us can risk getting involved. Everyone seems to have come to the same conclusion. Everyone is shocked by what they can see but no-one does anything to help. People cautiously edge forward and work their way around the fight to get out of the building as quickly as they can and I keep walking with them. The woman's out cold now but the kid is still pummelling her face. She's covered in her mother's blood . . .

The speed and number of people leaving the building is increasing rapidly. I can feel panic bubbling up under the surface and I keep moving, desperate to get out before it explodes. I look at the empty check-outs as I run past them and feel another momentary pang of guilt before pushing and shoving my way back out into the open and running towards my car. I throw the supplies into the back and then get in and lock the door.

I start the engine and look back at O'Shea's. Desperate people are flooding out of the ransacked shop now, tripping over each other to get away before the situation inside gets any worse. I stare at the building in disbelief, my head filled with images of my family and of what I've just witnessed. Could any of my children do what I've just seen to Lizzie or me? Worse than that, could we do it to any of them?

21

Lizzie asks me if I'm okay but I can't answer. I need to get back inside first. I need to get the food inside then shut the door and lock the bloody thing behind me and never open it again.

'Are you all right?' she asks again. 'Why were you so long?'

I run back to the car and grab the last few odds and ends that have fallen out of the rapidly disintegrating cardboard box. I push past her and throw the stuff into the kitchen.

'Dad,' Ed whines, 'can we have something to eat now? I'm starving . . .'

I ignore all of them and concentrate on locking the door and making sure my home and my family are secure.

'Move,' I grunt angrily at Ellis who is standing right in the middle of the hallway, stopping me from getting through.

'What's wrong?' Lizzie asks again from the other side of the kitchen table. When I don't answer she starts to unpack some of the food. She looks at what I've brought home and screws up her face. 'What did you get this for?' she says, holding up a jar of honey. 'None of us likes honey.'

All of the tension and fear that's been building up inside me this morning suddenly comes rushing to the surface. It's no-one's fault, I just can't help myself.

'I know no-one likes it,' I shout, 'no-one likes any of this fucking stuff but it's all I could get. You should go out there and see what it's like. It's madness out there. The whole bloody world is falling apart so don't start having a go at me and telling me that no-one fucking well likes honey.'

Liz looks like I've punched her in the face. She's gone white with shock. The kids are all in the kitchen with us now, staring at us both with wide, frightened eyes.

'I just . . .' she starts to say.

'I'm doing the best I can for us here,' I scream at her. 'There are people fighting on the streets. I've just watched a kid beating some

137

woman to death and no-one lifted a finger to help her, me included. It's fucking madness and I don't know what to do any more. The last thing I need is for you to start complaining and picking holes in what I've done when I feel like I've just risked my damn neck for you lot. I don't ask much, just some space and a little gratitude and understanding and . . .'

I stop shouting. Liz is trembling. She's standing there, back pressed against the cooker, and she's shaking with fear. What the hell is wrong with her? I take a single step around the table to get closer to her and she recoils. She slides further away from me, edging back towards the door. And then I realise what's wrong. Jesus, she thinks I've changed. She thinks I'm one of them. She thinks I'm a Hater.

'No, don't . . .' I start to say, trying to move closer again, 'Please, Lizzie . . .'

She's starting to sob. Her legs look like they're about to give way. Don't collapse on me, Liz, please don't . . .

'Stay back,' she says, her voice barely audible. 'Don't come any closer.'

I try to speak but I can't get the words out. Don't do this to me. I shuffle nearer.

'Stay back!' she screams again, sliding further along the wall away from me. She reaches the door and starts to push the kids out of the kitchen. She doesn't take her eyes off me.

'No, Liz,' I say, desperate to make her understand, 'please. I haven't changed. Please believe me. I'm sorry I shouted. I didn't mean to . . .'

She stops moving away but she's still unsure. I can see it in her eyes.

'If you're one of them I'll . . .'

'I'm not, Lizzie, I'm not. If I was one of them I'd have gone for you by now, wouldn't I?' I cry. I don't know what else to say. I'm starting to panic but I don't want her to see. 'Please, I'm not sick. I'm not like them. I'm calm. I was angry but I'm calm now, aren't I? Please . . .'

I can see that she's thinking hard about what I've just said. The children are peering around the door, trying to see what's happening. Inside I'm screaming but I force myself to stay level and not shout. My head is filled with all kinds of dark, terrifying thoughts. I just got angry, that's all. I'm not a Hater, am I?

'Okay,' she eventually mumbles, 'but if you shout at me like that again I'll—'

'I won't,' I interrupt. 'I forgot myself. I didn't think.'

I still don't know if she believes me. She's looking at me out of the corner of her eye and it's like she's waiting for me to attack her. I'd never hurt her. I'm relieved when she moves back round to the box of food and continues unpacking it. Every couple of seconds she looks up. Every time I move I see her catch her breath and stop.

'So what happened out there?' she asks, finally composed enough to be able to talk to me again. I don't know where to start. Between us we try and feed the kids while I explain about the queues at the supermarket and what I saw at O'Shea's. I tell her about the looting and about the girl attacking the woman and . . . and I realise again just how bad things have suddenly got.

Ellis is snapping at my heels. She's oblivious to the fact that anything's wrong. That's good, I decide. I'm glad. Now that she has her food she's nagging at me to let her watch a DVD. I follow her into the living room. She fetches the film she wants from the cupboard and brings it over. I switch on the TV but stop before I put the DVD in the machine.

'I turned that off about an hour ago,' Liz says. 'Couldn't stand watching any more of it. They keep showing the same thing again and again and again.'

I sit cross-legged in front of the television and stare at the pictures that flash in front of me. Christ, things are really bad. I've seen a lot of bizarre stuff over the last few days but what I'm watching now scares the hell out of me. Now I fully realise how dire and serious the situation has quickly become. The news has gone. There are no more reports and no more presenters. All we're left with is a continually repeated public information film. My stomach is churning with nerves again.

'Stay in your homes,' a deep and reassuring male voice announces over stock footage and a series of simplistic graphic images, back at the beginning of the loop again. 'Stay with your family. Stay away from people you don't know . . .'

I look up at Lizzie and she looks back at me and shrugs her shoulders.

'It's all just common-sense stuff. Nothing we haven't already heard.'

'Stay calm and don't panic.'

'What?' I protest. 'Stay calm and don't panic? Bloody hell, have they seen what's happening out there?'

'It gets better,' she says sarcastically. 'Listen to the next bit.'

'The authorities are working to bring the situation under control. Your assistance and cooperation is required to make sure this happens quickly and with as little disturbance as possible. Temporary controls and regulations are necessary to make this happen. Firstly, if you have to leave your home, you must carry some form of identification with you at all times. Secondly, with immediate effect an ongoing night-time curfew is in place. You may not travel between dusk and dawn. Anyone found on the streets after dark will be dealt with appropriately . . .'

Dealt with appropriately? Christ, what's that supposed to mean? Are they going to start locking people up for being out at night?

'Ensure that your home is secure. Prepare a safe room for you and your family to stay in. Ensure that the door to the safe room and all other access points can be secured and locked from the inside.'

'What the hell is this?' I say under my breath.

'Can you put my film on now please, Daddy?' Ellis moans impatiently.

'If any of the people you are with should begin to act aggressively or out of character, you must isolate yourselves from them immediately. Lock yourself and the rest of the people with you in your safe room. Remove the affected person from your property if it is safe to do so without putting yourself at risk. Remember that this person may well be a family member, a loved one or a close friend. They will be unable to control their actions and emotions. They will be violent and will show no remorse or understanding. It is vital that you protect yourself and those remaining with you.'

'Can you see why I turned it off?' Lizzie asks. 'This kind of thing is just making it worse.'

'I can't believe this . . .' I stammer, lost for words. 'I just can't believe this . . .'

'Think they know what's going on now?'

'I'm sure they do,' I answer. 'They must have worked it out if they're showing something like this. Someone must know what's happening, and that makes things even worse, doesn't it?'

'Does it? Why?'

I shrug my shoulders.

'Because things must be pretty well fucked if they're still not telling us anything. It sounds to me like they're trying to lock every-body down just to try and keep things under control, and what I've seen this morning makes me think that maybe things *aren't* under control right now.'

Lizzie frowns at me for swearing in front of Ellis. I turn back to the screen.

'. . . first indication will be a sudden fit of rage and anger,' the disturbingly unemotional voice on the TV continues. 'This rage will typically be directed at one person in particular. Remember that those affected may appear calm again once the initial outburst of anger and violence has passed. Continue to keep your distance. Regardless of who they are or what they say, these people are not in control of their actions. They will continue to pose a threat to you and your family . . .'

Lizzie strides past me and snatches Ellis's DVD from my hands. She shoves it into the machine and it starts to play.

'That's enough,' she snaps.

'I was watching that . . .'

'Will you go and get Dad?'

My heart sinks. I don't want to leave the flat again but I know I don't have any choice.

'When do you want me to . . . ?' I begin before she interrupts.

'Get him now,' she answers, nervously chewing her fingernails. 'If you won't go and get him I will.'

The thought of Lizzie being alone out there is worse than the thought of going out myself. I have to do it.

22

The lobby is silent. I shut the door to the flat behind me, lock it and cautiously look around. I've told Liz to make a safe room like they said on TV and then to shut herself and the kids in it. The living room is the obvious place. She's closed the curtains and they've turned the TV down low. From outside it looks like no-one's in.

I open the front door and cringe as the usual loud creaking sound echoes around the insides of the empty building.

'Is anyone there?' a voice called from the darkness upstairs. I freeze and try not to panic. What do I do? I want to keep moving and pretend I didn't hear anything but I can't. My family is in this building and I can't leave them knowing that someone else is in here with them. It could be anyone. They could be waiting for me to leave so they can get to Lizzie and the kids. But why would they have shouted out like that? I let the door go and it creaks again as it swings shut. I take a few slow steps back into the shadows and, for a second, I think about going back into the flat. I know that's not going to achieve anything. I have to go out and get Harry at some point.

'Who's there?' I hiss back, cursing myself for my stupidity. I'm acting like a character in a bad horror movie. You're supposed to run away from the monster, I tell myself, not move towards it.

'Up here,' the voice answers. I look up towards the top of the staircase and the first-floor landing. There's a face staring back at me from between the metal struts of the banister. It's one of the men from the flat on the top floor. I don't know whether it's Gary or Chris. I start cautiously to climb the stairs. I'm almost on the landing when the steps beneath my feet become tacky. The floor's covered in sticky puddles of blood. The man from the flat is lying on the ground in front of me, clutching his chest. He grunts and rolls over onto his back. His jeans and T-shirt are soaked through with blood. He turns his head to one side and manages to acknowledge me. He relaxes, relieved that someone's finally with him I suppose. He's in a real mess and I don't know where to start. Is there anything I can do for him or am I too late?

'Thanks, mate,' he gasps, propping himself up onto his elbows. 'I've been stuck here for hours. I heard someone come in a while back and I was trying to get . . .' He stops speaking and collapses and lies flat on his back again. The effort is too much. His voice gurgles and rasps. There must be blood in his throat. What am I supposed to do? Christ, I haven't got a clue how to try and help him.

'Do you want me to try and get you back upstairs?' I ask uselessly. He shakes his head and swallows to clear his throat.

'No point,' he groans as he tries to prop himself up again. I put my hand on his shoulder to keep him still. 'I want a drink,' he says. 'Can you go up to the flat and get me a beer?'

His eyes flutter for a second and I wonder if he's about to go. I get up quickly and climb the stairs to the top floor flat he shares with the other man. I follow a snail trail of dry blood along the hallway and into the living room of the flat which is otherwise surprisingly clean and well kept. Don't know why I expected anything else really. There's an upturned table in the middle of the room and next to it a smashed lamp. There's a video camera on a tripod next to a computer and a wide-screen TV. Looks like they enjoyed filming themselves here. There's an expensive-looking leather sofa and . . . and I realise that I'm standing here checking out the flat while one of its occupants lies dying at the bottom of the stairs. Forcing myself to move I go to the kitchen and grab a bottle of beer from the well-stocked fridge. I open it and run back down to the man on the first-floor landing.

'Here you go,' I say as I hold the bottle up to his mouth. I'm not sure how much he manages to swallow. Most of it seems to run down his chin. When I move the bottle away I see that its neck is covered in blood from his lips. What am I supposed to do now? I try to move him but it's no good. He moans with pain whenever I touch him. This poor bastard is dying as I'm watching and there's absolutely nothing I can do to help him. There's no point asking who did this to him or if there's anyone I can try and contact – the sudden exit of his lover / friend / business partner early this morning was a clear enough admission of guilt. I feel terrible as I stand next to him, trying to think of an excuse to leave as he lies dying at my feet. But what else can I do?

'I'll go and get help,' I say quietly, crouching down closer to him again, taking care not to get any of his blood on me. 'I'll go and find someone who'll be able to help you.'

He licks his blood-stained lips, swallows and shakes his head.

'Too late now,' he wheezes. Every move this poor sod makes is taking masses of effort and causing him huge amounts of pain. I wish he'd just shut up and lie still but he won't. He has something more to say. Exhausted, he turns his head towards me again and stares straight into my face.

'Just keep still and . . .' I start to say.

'I tried to get him,' he says breathlessly. 'Fucker had a knife on him just in case. He got me first.'

'What?'

'I tried to get him but he was ready for me . . .'

'What are you saying? Did he attack you? Was he a Hater?'

He shakes his head.

'You see everything so clearly when it happens to you. I had to kill him. It was him or me. I had to kill him before . . .'

I stand up and start to move away. Jesus Christ, is this the Hater? He's the one who started the trouble we heard last night. He's the one who lost control. Christ, I'm stood here wasting my time on a fucking Hater.

He licks his bloody lips again and swallows once more.

'It's them, mate,' he mumbles, 'not us. They're the ones who hate. Get yourself ready . . .'

I don't know what the hell he's talking about now and I don't want to hear any more. I need to get away from this sick piece of filth. I turn my back on him and run downstairs, safe in the knowledge that there's no way he'll be able to reach my family in the condition he's in. I think about finishing him off but that would make me as bad as them and I doubt whether I'd even be able to do it. I glance back and take one last look at the scum on the landing. He hasn't got long left. He'll be dead by the time I get back and it won't be a moment too soon.

I run out to the car and start the engine.

23

I can usually get from the flat to Harry's house in around fifteen minutes but it took almost an hour to get here today. There's still not a huge amount of traffic about but some roads are inaccessible. Some are backed-up with slow-moving queues, others have just been blocked off.

Harry's pretty shaken up like the rest of us although he won't admit it. He's subdued and much quieter than usual. Liz phoned him and told him I was coming to get him but he hasn't got anything ready. I'm upstairs with him now, helping him pack an overnight bag. He seems lost and helpless like a little kid. He keeps asking me questions he knows I can't answer. How long will I be away? What do I need to take? Will we be safe at your place?

Harry's house is quiet and dark. It's rare that I ever go upstairs. The place is small but it's still far too big for him alone. The rooms that Liz and her sister used to sleep in have been left untouched since they moved out and one side of Harry's bedroom is a shrine to Sheila, his late wife. She's been dead for three years but there are still more of her things in the bedroom than Harry's. The whole house is full of clutter. Old sod never throws anything out. He just can't let go.

I wanted to be in and out of here in minutes but Harry's delaying things again. I need to get back to Lizzie and the kids but I'm stood here watching him checking everything's switched off and then checking that he's checked everything. I want to tell him that I don't think it matters any more but that's only going to make things worse so I just humour him and try to hurry him along. My head is spinning. I really need to talk about what's happening but Harry's not the person I want to talk to. I don't know who is. I need to talk about the half-dead man on the landing and about what I saw in the convenience store this morning. I can't get the image of the kid beating her mother out of my head. Could one of our kids attack Lizzie like that? Could that be happening right now while I'm stood here wasting my time with this stupid old man? I bite my lip and try and stay calm. I can't show any emotion. I don't want Harry thinking I'm a Hater.

'Come on,' I say, interrupting him as he walks around the ground floor of his house, checking the windows and doors are locked for the third time, 'we need to get moving.'

I expect a sneering reply because that's what I usually get from Harry. He's a loud and opinionated old bugger who doesn't think much of me. He assumes he knows more than me about everything and he never takes kindly to being hurried or told what to do. I'm surprised when he just nods, picks up his bag and slowly walks towards the front door. I take the bag from him and put it in the car, leaving him to lock up his home.

'Quiet, isn't it?' he says as we drive back towards the flat. He immediately regrets his words as we pull onto a main road which is solid with traffic. We join the back of the queue. It's slow but it's still moving and I can't think of a better route home. I decide to sit tight.

'You okay, Harry?' I ask.

'Fine,' he mumbles. 'Bit tired, that's all.'

'Trouble sleeping?'

He nods his head.

'Something happened around the back of the house last night,' he explains, his voice quiet. 'There was a fight or an accident or something . . . lots of screaming, lots of noise . . .'

The traffic has slowed down again to almost a complete standstill. It's stop-start all the way.

'Don't know what's going on here,' I mumble.

The road we're crawling along runs past the front of a row of houses before swinging up and left over a bridge which spans the motorway below. As we follow the arc of the road the reason for the delay becomes apparent. There's a steady stream of cars leaving the motorway and rejoining the town traffic. We grind to a halt again midway over the bridge.

'What's the hold-up?' Harry asks, looking around curiously.

'No idea. Must have been an accident or something . . .'

'That's not an accident,' he says, peering out of his window and tapping his finger on the glass. I sit up in my seat and lean across him to try and see whatever it is he's looking at. There's a blockade of some kind stretching right across the motorway. There are dark green military juggernauts straddling both sides of the road. Armed guards are manning red-and-white-striped barrier gates while other soldiers direct the queues of approaching traffic. What the hell are they doing? Unless I'm mistaken, the cars trying to leave the city are being stopped. They're not even being searched. They're either being marshalled up the slip road and straight off the motorway or they're being sent round through a hole that's been cut in the central barrier and forced back the way they came. The traffic is being channelled back into town.

'Don't want us to go far, do they?' Harry says, watching the cars below us as we begin to shunt forward again.

'Thought they said they were getting things under control.'

'What?'

'I was watching something on the TV just before I came out to get you. They said the situation is being brought under control.'

'Well, this is probably part of that control, isn't it? They need to know where everyone is . . .'

'Do they?'

'How can the authorities protect us if they don't know where we are?'

I don't bother answering him. The fact that I've just seen a sub-stantial military presence out on the streets doesn't inspire me or fill me with confidence. If anything it makes me feel worse.

As we move away from the motorway the traffic begins to thin out again. I put my foot down and continue towards home.

My nervousness and paranoia are increasing by the second. I need to be back with my family.

The streets we're driving through now are uncomfortably silent and still. It all looks and feels perverse. The country seems to be tearing itself apart with unprecedented levels of violence, so why is everywhere so quiet? The normal human reaction to a threat like the Haters would be to stand and fight but today we can't. These people are sick. They're driven by a desire to kill and destroy and, from what I've seen, they won't stop until those desires have been satisfied. To stand and fight against them would mean displaying the same emotions as they do. It would be self-destructive. To fight back is to risk being called a Hater too. All we can do is keep ourselves to ourselves and not retaliate. The population is withdrawing from each other in fear. Fear of everyone else and fear of themselves.

We finally pull up outside the apartment block and I get Harry inside. I'm about to go back out to get his bag from the car when I spot a solitary figure walking down the street. Instinctively I wait in the shadows until I'm sure they've disappeared before setting foot out in the open again. Christ, I'm too scared to risk even being seen by anyone I don't know.

24

'**D**ad,' Ed says.

'What?' I grunt, annoyed that I've been interrupted. I've been reading through a pile of music magazines I found under the bed. I thought I'd thrown these out years ago. They've helped me get through the uneasy boredom of this never-ending afternoon.

'What's he doing?'

'What's who doing?' I ask, not lifting my head.

'That man from the house down the road. What's he doing?'

'What man?'

'Jesus Christ,' Lizzie screams as she walks into the room. The panic in her voice makes me drop my magazine and look up. Fucking hell, the man who lives in one of the houses adjacent to our apartment block is dragging his wife out of their house and into the middle of the street. She's a huge woman with a wide backside and flabby arms which are thrashing about wildly. The man – I think his name is Woods – is pulling her along by her feet and I can hear her screaming from here. He drags her down the kerb and her head cracks back against the road. He's carrying something else with him. I can't see what it is . . .

'What's he doing?' Ed asks again.

'Don't look,' Liz yells at him. She rushes across the room and tries to turn Ed around and push him towards the door. Josh is in the way. He's standing in the doorway eating a biscuit and Lizzie can't get past.

'Don't look at what?' Ellis asks. I didn't see her come in. She's behind me, standing on tiptoes and looking out of the window.

'Do what Mum says,' I say as I try to pull her away. She clings onto the windowsill and won't let go. The children have been going stir crazy trapped in the house. They're desperate for any distraction.

Outside Woods has stopped moving now. His wife is still lying on the ground and he's standing on her neck. Bloody hell, he's put his boot and his full weight on her throat. Her face is blood red and she's thrashing about more than ever but he's managing to keep her down even though he's half her size.

'Ellis, let go,' I shout as I finally manage to prise her away from the window. Ed is still watching and I can't help staring either. I can't look away. It was a bottle that Woods was carrying. He's unscrewed the lid now and he's emptying the contents all over his wife. What the hell is he doing?

'What's happening?' Harry asks. Now we're all in the living room. He's between me and the door and I have to move round him to get Ellis out. I try to close the curtains again but I can't reach from here. Harry's in the way.

'Get the children out of here,' Lizzie screams.

'Will you move, Harry?' I snap. 'I can't get through . . .'

I look out of the window again as Woods sets fire to his wife. Christ knows what he just doused her in but she's gone up in a huge ball of flames and the fire has caught him too. She's still moving. Bloody hell. I put my hands over Ellis's eyes but I'm slow to react and she's already seen too much. Woods trips away from the burning body, his trouser legs on fire. He staggers down Calder Grove but only makes it halfway down the road before he's consumed by the flames.

Between us we push the kids out into the hall. I go back to the living room.

Outside no-one does anything. No-one moves. There's no activity out on the street, not even when the fire from Woods's wife's burning body spreads and sets light to a pile of plastic sacks filled with rubbish which have been sat at the side of the road for more than a week. Thick black smoke billows up from the bags and from the corpses in the road, filling the air with dirty fumes.

Sobbing, Lizzie pulls the curtains shut.

The man on the landing at the top of the stairs is dead. I crept out of the flat a few minutes ago and went up to check. What a fucking horrible way to go – ending your days slowly bleeding to death on your own at the top of a dark, concrete staircase. Could I have done anything for him? Possibly. Should I have done anything for him? Definitely not. He was a Hater, and it's scum like him that have caused all of this. They're the reason everything is falling apart. They're the reason I've had to lock myself and my family in the flat. They're the reason we're all fucking terrified.

What scares me most about the body upstairs and what we saw on the street is the closeness of it all. I could cope with this crisis when it was just something on the news. I could even deal with it at the concert and when we saw the fight in the pub and the kid under the car. What's changed today is the proximity of the trouble to my children and my home. This flat felt safe until today.

25

The kids have definitely sensed a change now. Maybe it's because they've been trapped in the flat with no contact with anyone else for days. Obviously what they've seen today has made matters worse. They keep asking questions and I don't know how to answer them. I don't know what to say to them any more. I took the bolt I fixed on Sunday morning off the bathroom door and attached it to the inside of the living room (or 'safe room' as we're now supposed to call it) to try and make everyone feel a little safer. I don't know if it's done any good.

We've been sitting in the safe room for hours and I can't stand it any longer. I get up and wander aimlessly around the flat. I can't sit and do nothing, but there's nothing I can do either. I don't want to talk to anyone. I'm cold and tired and frightened. I walk into Josh and Ed's small room and climb up onto Ed's top bunk. His small-screen TV is at the end of the bed. I switch it on and flick through the channels. Nothing worth watching. There are a couple of channels showing repeats of old TV shows, the rest are just showing the public information film that we saw earlier. It's running at exactly the same time on all the major national channels. It must be produced and broadcast by the government. At least I assume it's the government. Who else could it be?

With nothing on TV and no other distractions I find myself looking out of the window just to the side of the bed. I lie down flat on my stomach on the narrow bunk and stare out through the net curtain at the street outside. From here I can see along the full length of Calder Grove – from the still smoking bodies of Woods and his wife right down to the junction of the road with Gregory Street. Apart from the drifting smoke everything else is still. The world feels silent and deserted, as if we've all been put in quarantine from each other. Now and again I catch sight of a lonely figure in the distance. People stick to the shadows and they're gone as quickly as they appear. There's hardly any other movement at all. Once in a while a car passes by, otherwise nothing else seems to move. It's like looking at a freeze-frame photograph of the world.

Why hasn't anyone done anything about the corpses? We've kept the curtains in the living room closed so the kids can't see them. If Woods's wife's body is still there in the morning I might go and throw a blanket over it just so it's out of view. I can see the blackened remains of the dead woman's arms. Her bony hands and fingers are lifted up and clasped together like she's praying or pleading for help.

I don't know what we're going to do. I'm trying not to panic. I don't think we have any choice but to lock ourselves in here and sit this thing out, however long that takes. I don't want to . . .

'What are you looking at?' a voice suddenly asks from beside me, making me jump. I look round and see that it's Ellis. She's crept into the bedroom and has managed to climb the ladder up to Ed's bed. She peers at me over the top rung with wide, saucer-shaped eyes.

'Nothing,' I answer, rolling over and giving her space to climb up with me. She puffs and pants and drags herself onto the bed.

'What are you doing in here?'

It's difficult to answer. I'm not exactly sure myself.

'Nothing,' I say again.

'You looking at the dead lady?' she asks in a remarkably innocent and matter-of-fact way.

'No, I'm just lying down for a while. I'm tired.'

'Why are you lying on Ed's bed? Why aren't you lying on yours and Mummy's bed?'

Her questions never seem to stop. I wish they would. I'm not in the mood to answer them.

'I wanted to watch the TV,' I tell her, not being entirely honest. 'I haven't got one in my bedroom.'

'Why not watch the other telly with the rest of us?'

'Ellis,' I say, stifling a yawn and pulling her closer, 'shut up, will you.'

'You shut up,' she mumbles under her breath. She yawns too and shuffles closer to me.

For a little while the room is quiet again and I begin to wonder whether Ellis has fallen asleep. But it's not just this room that's quiet – the whole flat is ominously silent. In the distance I can just about hear the muffled sounds of the TV in the living room. Are they being quiet or is there something wrong with the others? Is it because of what's happening outside, or is the isolation and uncertainty starting to have an effect on the rest of my family? Is one of them about to start changing, or have they already changed . . . ? I find myself thinking about what's happening outside again and I'm depressed by a constant stream of dark and uncomfortable thoughts. Surely things can't continue like this indefinitely? There has to come a point when something gives or the situation resolves itself, doesn't there? I don't have any answers and I'm actually relieved when Ellis decides to attack me with another barrage of much easier questions.

'Will we be going back to school tomorrow?' she asks naively.

'I don't think so,' I reply.

'The next day?'

'I don't know.'

'The next day?'

'I don't know. Look, Ellis, we don't know when school's going to be open again. Hopefully it won't be too long.'

'I'm going on a trip next week.'

'I know.'

'My class is going to a farm.'

'I know.'

'We're going on a coach.'

'I know.'

'Will we still be able to go?'

'I hope so.'

'Will you take me if school's still shut?'

'I'll take you.'

She seems happy with that and, again, she becomes quiet. I lie back and close my eyes. The day so far has been long and emotionally draining and it has taken its toll. My eyes feel heavy. In just a few short minutes I feel Ellis's body go limp in my arms. Her breathing changes, becoming shallow and steady and I look down at her. She's dozing, completely relaxed and almost asleep. In a world which has suddenly become completely irrational, unpredictable and fucked-up she remains perfect and unaltered. This little girl means everything to me.

I'm tired. I close my eyes.

I was almost asleep for a second until the image of the girl in the supermarket this morning returned. For a terrifying moment I imagined that it was Ellis, and that she was attacking Lizzie lying on the ground. I'm frightened. I'm petrified by the prospect that whatever it is that's happening outside will eventually find its way into my home and harm my family.

I try to imagine this beautiful little girl attacking me.

I try to imagine me attacking her.

26

It's just before midnight. The children are asleep. We're sitting in the living room in silence and in almost total darkness. Harry, Liz and I couldn't be sitting any further apart from each other in here. Harry's opposite the window, looking out through half-drawn curtains. Liz is by the door, staring into space. The television has been off all night. No-one's saying anything new so there's no point watching. The lack of information is just making things worse.

'Anyone want a drink?' I offer. This silence is unbearable.

'Not for me,' answers Harry. I look over at Lizzie. She shakes her head and looks down. She hasn't spoken for hours. We had a conversation about the kids just after they'd gone to bed but since then she's hardly said anything.

The room is filled with dull, rumbling noise and a sudden flash of light as a huge ball of flame mushrooms up into the sky from a building nearby.

'What in hell's name was that?' Harry grumbles as he gets up from his chair and staggers to the window. He pulls the curtains fully open and I stand behind him and look over his shoulder. I can't see what's burning. It looks like it might be the medical centre on Colville Way. It's about quarter of a mile away from here but that's too close for comfort. As the initial noise and burst of flame dies down I hear other, equally frightening sounds. A desperate woman yells out for help. Her voice is hoarse and terrified. She's pleading with someone, screaming at them to get away from her and leave her alone and . . . and her cries suddenly stop. Now I can hear a car starting. The engine is revved and accelerated furiously. The car begins to move at speed but its brief journey is over in seconds. Brakes squeal and tyres skid across the road before I hear the unmistakable thump and crunch of a collision.

The quiet which follows the sudden mayhem is a thousand times worse than the flames and the screams. I'm standing here waiting to hear sirens as the police, fire brigade or anyone who can help reaches the scene but there's nothing, just a cold and empty silence. I know that the response would be the same if anything happened here. We're completely on our own.

I turn around. The room is still filled with dull light from the fire and I can see that Lizzie's crying. I sit down next to her leaving Harry at the window watching the inferno in the near distance. I put my arm around her and pull her closer.

'Come on,' I say uselessly. She doesn't react. I reach out and hold her hand but it just sits limply in mine.

'It should never have got to this stage,' Harry chunters with his back to us, standing at the window like a general surveying the battlefield. 'They should never have let it come to this.'

He turns round and stares at us both, seeming to be almost demanding a response. Liz stares back at him, her face streaked with tears.

'Leave it, Harry,' I warn him. 'This isn't the time . . .'

'When is the time then?' he snaps. 'When do you want to start talking about it? When the trouble reaches your front door?'

'There's a body in the street about ten metres away. I'd say it's reached the front door already,' I snap back angrily.

'So what are we going to do about it?' he demands. There's an uncomfortable hint of panic and desperation in his raised voice. 'Are we just going to sit here? Are we just going to . . . ?'

'What can we do?' I interrupt, holding Lizzie's hand a little tighter. 'What are the options, Harry? Should we sit here and keep ourselves and the children safe, or do you want us to go out there and join in the fighting?'

'That's what caused the problems in the first place,' he argues.

'Exactly, so what else are we supposed to do?'

Harry is pointing his finger at me now and his voice is getting louder. He's not making any sense and I'm biting my lip, trying not to panic. Once again I find myself wondering if he's about to turn.

'This is just what people have been waiting for,' he continues at an uncomfortable volume, 'an excuse to fight. Not that they've needed much of an excuse before, but now it doesn't matter. People can do what the bloody hell they like without fear of any repercussions. It's a chance for the scum around here to show their true colours and . . .'

'Shut up,' Lizzie yells angrily. 'Just shut up, Dad. You're not helping.'

'These people need a firm hand,' he rants, oblivious. He points accusingly at the TV. 'And if the idiots running the television stations hadn't sensationalised things by showing more and more violence then maybe we wouldn't be in this mess. If there had just been some respect for authority maybe we'd all be . . .'

'There is no authority any more,' I shout back. 'I saw a policeman shooting people in cold blood yesterday and then I watched other officers turn their weapons on him and gun him down. The authorities are as screwed as the rest of us.'

'But if people would just stop . . .'

'For Christ's sake, shut up!' Liz screams again. She snatches her hand from mine and storms out of the room. I watch her disappear down the hallway and almost immediately the paranoia begins. Harry is quiet now – is it Liz who's turning? Is she heading for the kids' rooms? Is she going to hurt them? I get up and run after her. I'm relieved when I find that she's shut herself in the bathroom and I feel stupid and guilty for thinking she could have been doing anything else. I slowly trudge back to the living room where Harry finally seems to be calming down.

'She all right?' he grunts.

I nod but I can't bring myself to speak to him. He turns his back on me again and continues to watch the smoke rising from the building burning on Colville Way.

FRIDAY

27

Not sure what time I finally went to sleep. I lay on the bed for hours trying (and failing) to make sense of everything that's happening. I must have looked at the alarm clock a hundred times or more in the night. I watched every hour tick by . . .

'Dad.'

I'm still half asleep but Ed wakes me up. I sit up quickly. What's wrong? What's happened? I rub my eyes and try to focus on my son's face. The room's dark but I think he's okay. I look down and see that Lizzie's still sleeping next to me in bed. She seems okay too.

'Dad,' he says again, annoyed that I haven't answered.

'What's the matter?' I mumble. 'Are the others all right?'

He nods. What he wants to tell me has obviously got nothing to do with Ellis or Josh.

'The telly's bust,' he grunts.

I slump back on my pillow, relieved. Is that all? Thank God for that.

'What's the matter with it?' I ask, struggling to sound interested.

'Can't get a picture.'

'Is it plugged in?'

'Yes,' he groans, 'I'm not stupid.'

I'm too tired to pick him up for being rude.

'Have you checked the cables at the back?'

'I haven't touched them. It was working yesterday, wasn't it?'

'What about the telly in your bedroom?'

'Can't get the channel I want on my telly. Come on, Dad, get up.'

'I'll come and have a look in a couple of minutes,' I yawn. 'Let me stay here for a bit longer . . .'

'But my programme's on now,' he protests. 'Please, Dad.'

I close my eyes for a few seconds longer but it's obvious that I'm not going to get any peace until Ed's got the TV fixed. Cursing under my breath I get up and stumble across the cold bedroom floor and down the hallway, side-stepping Harry as I meet him by the kitchen door. Ed follows then pushes past me as we reach the living room. He picks up the remote control and switches on the TV.

'See . . .' he says, flicking through the channels.

I sit and stare at the screen.

'What's the matter?' Harry asks, as he wearily drags himself into the room after us.

'Telly's broke,' Ed tells him.

'It's not broken,' I say as I flick through the channels.

'Have you checked the aerial?' Harry suggests.

'There's nothing wrong with it,' I tell them both, 'look.'

Harry moves around so that he can see the screen. And now he can see why I've been staring. It's the same thing on every channel. A black screen with stark white text.

REMAIN CALM.

DO NOT PANIC.

TAKE SHELTER.

WAIT FOR FURTHER INSTRUCTIONS.

THE SITUATION IS UNDER CONTROL.

28

It's eleven o'clock and Lizzie, Harry and the kids are sitting in the living room. There's something happening outside. The others haven't noticed yet. I don't want the children and Liz getting upset again so I haven't said anything to anyone. It started about half an hour ago. I've heard heavy vehicles moving in the distance and the occasional scream or shout. I've also heard gunfire.

I've tried looking through every window in the flat but I can't see what's going on out there. I have to know. I make sure the others are all distracted then creep out of the apartment. I stop halfway across the lobby. Everything looks just as it did when I was out here yesterday but today the building feels different because of what's upstairs. I stop at the bottom of the staircase and, just for a second, I think about turning round and going back into the flat again. I'll get a better view from the flats on the other floors but I'm worried about going upstairs. I don't think there's anyone else up there – the car belonging to the people on the top floor is still missing and I can't hear anything. But what about the body? I know the man on the landing is dead but have I got the balls to pass his corpse? My head is suddenly filled with stupid nightmare images of his lifeless hands reaching out to grab me. The sound of another gunshot in the distance spurs me into action. I take a deep breath and run up the stairs, not stopping until I've reached the flat on the top floor. I peer in through the half-open door to make sure it's still empty then step inside.

There are only two floors between our flat and this one but the view from up here is completely different. Those extra few feet of height make all the difference and from here I can see for miles around. I can see almost all of our estate and I can see the city centre in the distance. This morning the world looks like the TV footage that gets sent home by war correspondents. The skyline is dark and grey. Dirty, thick smoke is climbing from the blackened shells of burnt-out buildings. There's nothing much left of the medical centre on Colville Way. The streets are deserted.

How am I supposed to protect my family from this? I can sense the danger increasing almost by the second and there's nothing I can do to stop it. I think of the kids downstairs and I feel terrified and helpless. They're depending on me and I don't know what I can do to keep them safe.

I can see movement in the distance now. Can't see exactly what it is from here. I turn around and grab the video camera I saw when I was up here yesterday. Christ knows what the men who lived here used it for. I've got no interest in finding out. I take the camera over to the window and switch it on. There's hardly any battery power left. I find the zoom lens control and set it so that it's focused as far as possible into the distance. It takes me a few seconds to aim the camera in the right direction and to relocate the movement I've just seen.

I think I'm looking at the area around Marsh Way but I'm not sure. Whatever the name of the road I'm watching is, there are two large green-grey trucks driving along it. On either side of the trucks are lines of uniformed figures. Bloody hell, they're armed soldiers wearing what looks like full battle gear. They have masks or visors obscuring their faces. The trucks stop midway along the street and the guards which surround them split into smaller groups. Some remain close to the back of the vehicles while others move towards the houses on either side of the road. From here I can only see one group of figures clearly but I guess they're all doing the same thing. It looks like a house-to-house inspection.

The trooper at the front of the group hammers his fist on the door. Christ, they're not waiting to be invited inside. Four of the soldiers in the group of five force their way into the house as soon as the door is opened. The fifth uniformed figure follows them inside carrying something. It's difficult to keep the camera focused from this distance and I can't tell whether it's a clipboard or one of those tablet computer things he's holding. They all disappear into the building and I wait for them to re-emerge. And I wait. And I wait.

Elsewhere along the street the same thing is happening. Groups of soldiers are splintering away from the trucks and are checking each house in turn. I look up from the video-camera viewfinder screen for a second and catch sight of more movement in another road nearby. Same thing's happening again. I squint as the sun breaks through the heavy cloud for the first time today and I can see at least two more clusters of trucks and soldiers working their way along other streets, all within a few hundred metres radius of each other. I focus back on the house I was originally watching in Marsh Way as the five soldiers march back out and immediately turn their attention to the building next door, leaving a dazed and bewildered middle-aged couple to timidly close their front door behind them.

There are helicopters flying over the town. Strange. Maybe they're coordinating the movements of the troops on the ground?

The soldiers I've been watching have forced their way into another house now. They reappear in less than a minute, this time dragging someone behind them. I can't make out whether it's a man or a woman but they're kicking and punching and doing all they can to get away. I can see that it's a woman now. She's only half-dressed. They've turned her around and they're marching her towards the nearest truck. She's still fighting. As they push her towards the back of the vehicle she somehow manages to free herself from the soldiers' hold. She starts to run down the road and . . . and now I can't believe what I'm seeing. One of the soldiers steps forward and raises his rifle. Instead of chasing after her he simply shoots her in the back. Two of them pick up the fallen body and throw it unceremoniously into the back of one of the trucks.

They must finally be flushing out the Haters. Thank God for that.

It's about time. I hope the bastards get everything they deserve.

29

It's a relief knowing that someone finally appears to be taking control of the situation. The soldiers on the streets are the first indication we've had that the authorities are at last doing something to help us. I'm glad, but I'll be happier when they've been and gone from here. I don't say anything to the others. I don't want the kids and Lizzie getting upset again.

My head is spinning. I'm finding it harder and harder to cope with being trapped inside the safe room with the rest of the family. This intense claustrophobia is killing me. We've been sat together for hours and hardly anyone has spoken apart from the children who fight and bicker constantly. I know they can't help it but they're really beginning to piss me off. Lizzie and Harry don't seem bothered by them. Maybe it's just me. Maybe it's the thought of the soldiers outside. I'm getting increasingly anxious sitting here waiting for the inevitable knock at the door.

I use going to the toilet as an excuse to get up and get out of the room. I close the living room door behind me and lean up against it, relieved. The atmosphere in there was oppressive and the air out here is much cooler and fresher. I stumble down the hallway and pause at the front door. Should I go upstairs and check the streets again? What if the army is here already? How would it look if I opened the door and ran head first into one of those patrols? They might think I was a Hater. Would they give me any chance to explain before aiming their rifles at me?

I use the toilet then traipse towards Ed and Josh's room. I climb up onto Ed's bed like I did yesterday and stare out of the window for a while. I can't see anything. If I ignore the bodies then everything looks quiet, still and relatively normal out there. It's deceptive. Under the surface the whole world is tearing itself apart.

My head hurts. I'm tired of thinking constantly about everything that's happening. I just want to switch off for a while.

I roll over onto my back, close my eyes and wait for the knock at the door.

30

I hear movement inside the flat, away from the safe room. Don't know how long I've been lying here on my own. Must have fallen asleep. I feel sick. I need to get a drink. I sit up, swing my legs out over the side of the bunk and climb down. My body aches as I stretch and stumble down the hallway.

Someone's in the kitchen. I move closer and see through the open door that it's Harry. He's standing at the sink with his back to me, making a drink or washing up or something. I take a step through the door and into the room with him and then stop. Don't know why. Something's not right. I don't want to go any closer. I can taste something in the air and it makes me feel uneasy. No, it's more than that, it makes me feel unsafe. Harry stops what he's doing. Does he know I'm here? For what feels like for ever neither of us moves. Then he slowly turns around. Is he . . . ?

Jesus Christ. I stare deep into the old man's eyes and I am frozen to the spot with fear. Can this be the same man? He glares back at me with cold, steely eyes filled with an inexplicable hate and disgust. I can sense his revulsion of me coming off him like a stench and I know that for some inexplicable but undeniable reason he wants me dead. He wants to destroy me. My legs become weak with nerves as I realise that the hate has finally arrived in my home.

Harry moves suddenly and I react at speed. He takes just a single step forward but it's enough and I know that my life is in danger unless I act now. An overwhelming instinctive desire for self-preservation takes over as I move away from him. I look over to my right. On the worktop is our wooden knife block. I grab the black-handled bread knife and pull it from the block like I'm unsheathing a sword. In a single movement I charge towards Harry and plunge it deep into his flesh, just above his waist. I put my other arm around him and pull him closer to me, forcing the blade deeper and deeper into his gut, twisting it round as I push it forward. I feel its serrated edge slice through his skin and cut through muscles, veins and arteries and I shove it deeper into him until the entire length of the knife has disappeared. I feel a sudden flow of hot blood as it gushes out over my hand and I let go of the knife and push Harry away. He trips back. His legs buckle beneath him and he collapses to the floor, smacking the back of his head against the oven door as he falls. I stand over him. He's still breathing but he won't last long now. I have to be sure that he's dead.

There's a scream from the doorway – a shrill, ear-piercing yell – and I turn around and see Lizzie and the children. She looks at me with the same cold expression as her father and I sense the hate again. I pull the knife out from the dying man's gut and lunge towards her, knowing that she has to die too. She backs away, dragging the children out of the room with her. Edward and Josh stare angrily at me with as much hate as their mother.

'Daddy!' Ellis screams. I look deep into my little girl's face and I know instantly that she's not like the others. She's like me. She hasn't changed. I run around the edge of the kitchen table and reach out for her but I'm too late. Her mother has already grabbed her by the scruff of her neck and has pulled her out of reach. Her tiny, tear-streaked face is filled with fear and shock and her eyes bulge wide as Liz yanks on her clothing, hauling her away from me. Ed glares at me. Even Josh despises me. My sons despise me and I know that I have to destroy them too.

I hurl myself towards Lizzie again, knowing that I have to kill her before she can hurt me and before she can harm Ellis. She shouts at the children to move and they run down the hallway towards the living room. Edward pulls Josh's pushchair across the hall and I trip over it, ending up on my hands and knees. Before I can get up and get to the living room they slam the door shut. I hear the bolt click across.

What the hell do I do now? How did this happen? How could my family turn against me so quickly? I have to forget about them and get to Ellis. She hasn't changed and I know that she needs me. I pick myself up and run at the door. I smash my shoulder into it but it doesn't move. I run back and charge it again and again and, the fifth time I hit it, I feel the bolt give way. I try to force the door open but it only moves a couple of inches. They've pushed furniture against it to stop me from getting inside. Why are they doing this to me?

I hammer my fists against the door.

'Ellis,' I shout. 'Ellis!'

I can hear her. She's trapped in there. I can hear her screaming back at me. She's like me, not them, and she needs to be with me. She's not safe in there. I'm desperate. I can't leave her. I throw myself at the door again and the force of the impact shakes my whole body to the core.

'Ellis!' I yell again. I can still just about hear her muffled reply.

There has to be another way to get to her. The window. I'll get in through the living room window. I turn and run back down the hallway, past the body in the kitchen and out into the lobby. I push the front door open and burst into the cold, rain-soaked world outside. Now that I'm out in the open I'm aware of noise all around me. I can hear the helicopters, the military trucks, gunshots and the sounds of people like me fighting to survive. It's like being in the middle of a war zone. But this isn't the noise of one war being fought, it's hundreds of separate clashes. Hundreds, probably thousands of battles fought by people like me who've been turned on and betrayed.

I'm at the living room window. I look inside. Lizzie is still piling furniture against the door. Edward spots me almost immediately and Lizzie shoves the children into the corner of the room. Ellis is trapped behind Edward and Josh but I can still see her. I can still see her face. She's crying and mouthing my name.

I look around for something to use to smash the glass. There's a broken paving slab halfway down the path to the front door. I pick it up and manage to throw it through the window. The glass shatters and the noise is uncomfortably loud. I can hear their voices again now. I can hear Lizzie screaming at them to keep back and keep away from me. I drag myself up and climb through the window frame, feeling shards of glass digging into me and slicing my skin. The pain doesn't matter.

I force my body through the window head first and collapse onto the carpet. I quickly get up but my footing is unsteady and I'm off balance. Lizzie is running towards me. She has something in her hands – it's the metal tube from the vacuum cleaner. She swings it at me. I try to duck out of the way but I'm too slow and she hits me.

A sudden burning, searing pain across my face.

Blood pouring from my nose and into my mouth.

Face down on the carpet. I can't . . .

31

The living room is cold and silent. I slowly prise open my eyes. I don't think there's anyone else here. The pile of furniture has been moved and the door is open. Rain is blowing in through the smashed window and the backs of my legs are wet. I try to sit up but the pain is too much and I let myself fall back down again.

How long have I been lying here?

I start to remember what happened. I work my way backwards. I remember Lizzie hitting me. I remember the look of hatred on her face, matched only by the similar expressions on Edward and Josh's faces. I close my eyes and try to pull myself together. Watching my partner and children run from me and knowing that they have such hate for me hurts more than the physical pain I'm now feeling. I feel empty, betrayed and scared. I can't explain anything that's happened. I don't know why I killed Harry, I just know that I had to do it. I can't explain why almost my entire family turned against me so quickly and so completely. I can't explain why Ellis didn't turn either. Christ, I have to find her.

I force myself to get up. My body hurts and every movement is difficult. Very slowly, using the arm of the sofa for support, I manage to stand. I catch sight of myself in the mirror that hangs over the gas fire. My right eye is black and swollen. One of my front teeth is loose and I can taste blood at the back of my throat. When I see the state of my face I start to really feel the pain. I drag myself into the kitchen and step over the body on the floor to get myself some water.

That's better.

The water is ice-cold and refreshing and it helps clear some of the dullness from my spinning head. I stand over the sink and wash my mouth out, spitting blood into the bowl. I stare into the pinky-red water and try not to look at Harry lying dead at my feet.

What the hell happened? The kitchen floor is covered with his dark crimson blood. His lifeless eyes stare up towards the ceiling and I can feel them burning into me. I don't regret what I did – I had to kill him before he killed me – I just need to understand why . . .

I turn off the tap and, apart from the occasional drip of water, the flat is otherwise silent. Could Lizzie have taken the children and hidden upstairs in one of the other apartments? I slowly walk towards the kitchen door, listening carefully. I know in my heart they've gone.

Fuck.

A sudden realisation hits me like a punch to the guts, more painful even than the physical and emotional blows I've already taken. Thinking about the flats upstairs has made me remember the body on the landing and the Hater's words to me when he lay there dying. 'Be ready for them,' he said to me, 'it's them, not us. You see everything clearly when it happens to you.' Jesus Christ, he looked at me and saw another Hater. I'm one of them. It's the only logical explanation. How could Harry, Lizzie, Edward and Josh all change at the same time? It stands to reason that I'm the only one who is any different. I can't explain how or why, but when I looked into their eyes I knew immediately that the others weren't like me and that they were a threat. I sensed revulsion coming off them. I looked at my family and I feared them and that explains why I did what I did and why so many others have killed before me. I had to attack them before they attacked me. All except Ellis . . .

Keep calm I try to tell myself as I run down the hallway and go out into the lobby. I look out through the front door. Damn, my car has gone. Bloody hell, they've taken the car and now they could be anywhere. I'm struggling to think straight and my panic-induced nausea has returned. Keep calm, I say to myself again. Think logically. Where would they have gone? Their options are limited. They could have gone to Harry's house but that's un-likely with him lying dead on the kitchen floor. Most probably Lizzie will have taken them to her sister's place. I'll look for them there.

I'm cold. My clothes are wet and are soiled with both Harry's blood and my own. I'll get changed, get some things together and then go and find Ellis. I don't know where we'll go once I get her back. We can't come back here. This place isn't safe any more.

32

I'm washed and changed and ready to go but I can't bring myself to leave. The reality of what has happened is finally hitting home. The adrenaline and nervous fear has disappeared and now I'm left feeling empty, confused and scared.

I've realised I've lost everything.

I'm standing in Edward and Josh's bedroom now just looking around. It's too painful . . . I can't put into words how this is making me feel. I know that my boys are within touching distance but somehow I also know that they're gone and I'll never be with them again. I pick up a toy – a piece of nothing, just a cheap plastic hamburger meal giveaway gift – and it fills me with pain. Josh had this about three weeks ago. Harry gave us some money. We were out late and we filled the kids up with fast food. It was the first time Josh had had a meal to himself. He was so proud of it. He spent more time playing with this bloody toy than he did eating his burger.

I have to let them go.

I go through to the bedroom that Lizzie and I shared and I pick the bag I've packed up off the bed. The wardrobe door is open. I look along Lizzie's clothes rail and all the different outfits I see remind me of so many times. It fills me with a gut-wrenching sadness. All the memories I have – every second of the life I've led since I first met her – suddenly means nothing.

It would have been easier if they'd died. I know what I am now, and I know that Lizzie, Edward and Josh are different. I don't understand the differences between us, but I know beyond any doubt that they are insurmountable. I know that I'll never be with my partner and children again. As for Ellis . . . she's like me and I'll fight with my last breath to get her back.

I'm trying to shift the body in the kitchen. In spite of the hate I saw in Harry's eyes I don't want to leave him like this –

half-dressed and twisted and slumped in the corner of the room. I pull his feet to try and straighten him out but his limbs are stiff and unresponsive. I fetch a duvet from the bedroom and drape it over the corpse.

While I'm trying to move the body there's a noise. I get up and run to the living room to look out of the broken window. Two army trucks have pulled into the road and I know that I have to get out of here quickly. I don't know for sure any more whether these soldiers will help me or turn against me but I can't take any chances. What about the woman I saw shot dead in the street earlier this morning? Was she like me or like the others? Was she a Hater too?

Move. Get moving now and don't stop. But where do I go? The trucks are getting closer. I swing my bag up onto my shoulder and run out of the flat and into the lobby. Where now? Will they check the flats upstairs? Could I risk hiding there? I know I have to get myself away from here and I sprint towards the rear exit. I try to open the fire door but it's padlocked shut. Christ, how long has it been like that? What would have happened to Lizzie and the kids if there'd been a fire? Doesn't matter now. I look back and I can see movement right outside the apartment block. They're coming. Keep moving. Just keep moving.

The door to the other ground-floor flat is open. I'm inside it now and it stinks. No-one's lived here officially for the last six months but it's been used regularly by tramps, junkies, dossers and God knows who and what else. Its layout is a mirror image of my flat. I run through to the kitchen and force the window above the sink open. I can hear soldiers inside the building now. I can hear their heavy booted footsteps in the lobby. I scramble through the window and jump down into the overgrown communal back garden. I'm out. Without thinking I run through the long grass to the end of the garden then quickly scramble up the muddy bank which separates our block from the gardens of the privately owned houses which back onto us. I run along the ends of the gardens until I reach a tall wooden fence. I have to try and climb over it. I drag myself up, the muscles in my arms burning with effort, and manage to swing one leg over the top of the fence. I flick myself over and fall onto the pavement on the other side, landing painfully among the dog shit, litter and weeds. I stand up, brush myself down and run on.

33

The safest place to hide, I decide as I sprint, is somewhere I know the soldiers have already been. I double back on myself and head down the road which runs parallel with Calder Grove before cutting across a couple more streets and finally reaching Marsh Way. This is the area where I saw the soldiers patrolling when I watched from the top-floor window this morning.

The road is empty. There's no sign of the military presence I saw here earlier. I stand in the shadows under a tree at the end of the street and look up and down. There's no sign of any kind of presence at all. Everything is completely still. Nothing's moving here now. Nothing except me.

I notice that the front door of one of the houses on the other side of the road has just opened slightly. I run towards it and push my way inside. I meet the owner of the house dragging a bag of rubbish down the hall, about to throw it out. He looks up and I know immediately that he's not like me. I have to kill him.

'Who the hell are you . . . ?' he starts to say. I throw myself at him, grabbing him by the scruff of his neck and pushing him further back into the house. I keep moving, feeling strong and in control but not knowing where I'm going or what I'm doing. We trip into a filthy kitchen and I slam him against a wall cupboard. His body rocks back with the impact. He struggles and tries to fight me off but I know I can kill him. I have strength, speed and surprise on my side. I put my hand over his face, grip tight and smash his head back against the cupboard door. He's still fighting. I pull his head forward and smash it back again, harder this time. And again. Once more and still harder, so hard now that I feel something crack – not sure if it's the door or his skull. Again and he stops fighting. Again and he slumps down. Again and it's done.

I drag the body across the floor and leave it lying out of the way in the corner of the kitchen. Then I close and lock the door and finally stop to catch my breath and plan my next move.

I've never felt like this before. Part of me still feels devastated and empty because of what's happened to me today. Part of me suddenly feels stronger and more alive than I ever have before. The way I killed the owner of this house was so out of character and yet it felt right and it felt good. I feel like I could take on a hundred thousand of them if I have to.

I am a Hater.

Sat here in one of the bedrooms of this untidy and squalid little house I've finally managed to fully accept that I am a Hater. The title seems so wrong now but I can understand why it was originally given. To those on the outside – those who haven't felt what I'm feeling now – our actions could easily be misinterpreted as being driven by hate. But they're not. Everything I have done today has been in self-defence. I have killed to prevent myself from being killed. Those people, those 'normal' people, are the ones who create the hate. I can't explain it. I can see it in their eyes and I can almost taste it in the air around them. It's like a sixth sense, an instinct. I sensed it coming off Harry and that was why I killed him. It was the same with the man downstairs and it'll be the same with the next one I meet. I'll keep going and I'll keep killing for as long as I have to.

And now I finally begin to see where this is going. At last I'm starting to understand why this whole crisis has seemed so endless and directionless from the outset. It's us against them. There's not going to be a drawn match or a ceasefire or any political negotiations to resolve this. There won't be an end to this fighting until one side has prevailed and the enemy lies dead at their feet.

It's kill or be killed.

Hate or be hated.

The light is beginning to fade and I'm ready to move. I've waited until now hoping I'll gain a little cover and protection from the darkness. I take some food from the kitchen (there's hardly anything worth salvaging) and am ready to head back out into the open.

In the short time I've spent in this house my mood and emotions have been swinging and changing constantly. Half of me feels excited and alive because of what I have become. Part of me feels free and unrestrained for the first time in as long as I can remember and I'm relieved to have finally walked away from the parts of my life I detested. I feel physically strong, determined and full of energy and yet all of this counts for nothing in the moments that I find myself thinking about the past. Lizzie and I would have been together for ten years next year. We've brought our children up together and, although we've had our moments, we've always been close. All of that has gone now and it hurts. I may be a Hater, but I still feel pain. I wish that Liz, Edward and Josh could have changed too. I have to stop thinking about them. I'm struggling to make sense of my emotions. I still love them but at the same time I know that if I had to I'd kill them in an instant.

As I walk through the house something catches my eye.

In the living room, on a small round table next to a dirty, threadbare and obviously well-used armchair, is a booklet. A government-produced booklet. It looks clean and new and yet it's strangely familiar. I pick it up and start to leaf through its pages. I remember receiving something similar through the door a few months back when there was some terrorist threat or other. The booklet is pretty generic, telling the public what action to take in the event of an emergency. It covers bomb threats and natural disasters, that kind of thing. It tells people to stay in their homes and tune in to the radio or TV for updates. It's also got information about administering basic first aid, what supplies to maintain and emergency contact details. At the back are several pages full of propaganda and rubbish – how the country is prepared for all eventualities and how the emergency services will spring into action at the drop of a hat, that kind of garbage. There are some loose pages that have been added to the guide, and when I look at them I realise that this booklet was most probably given to the owner of this house by the military after their visit / inspection / clean-up operation today. The absence of any real facts is un-surprising and it immediately smells like more political bullshit. Still, it's interesting to read what they're finally telling the rest of the population about people like me.

The pages talk about what's happened to us as being an illness. It implies that this is some kind of infection or disease that causes a form of dementia but it skirts around the issue and doesn't use such direct language or present any hard facts. It says that a small proportion of the population – they suggest no more than one in a hundred people – are susceptible to 'the condition'. It talks about symptoms, saying that people who are affected will become delirious and will, at random, attack people violently and irrationally. Fucking idiots. There's nothing random or irrational about what I've done today.

What bothers me most of all is what I read on the final extra page. The booklet explains how affected people are being rounded up and taken away and 'treated'. It doesn't take a genius to work out that's the reason for the trucks and the soldiers working their way through town. So what does this so-called treatment involve? From what I've seen it's limited to a bullet in the back of the head.

I'm wasting my time. I don't want to read any more. I shove the booklet into my bag and, after checking the street outside is empty, I leave the house and its dead owner behind. I'll make my way across town to Liz's sister's house and bring Ellis home.

I feel strong. Superior to all of the people who haven't changed. I'm glad that I'm the one in a hundred. I'd rather be like this than like them.

34

I feel like I've been running for miles but I've slowed down now. I've reached the edge of town and there are fewer buildings and shadows to hide in. I don't want to be seen. I could have taken a car but there's nothing else on the roads now and I would have drawn too much attention to myself. I've lost track of time. It's early evening and the light has almost completely gone. I'm cold, soaked through by the heavy rain that's been falling for the last hour or so, but that's just a minor physical discomfort and I still feel surprisingly strong.

I don't know how long I've been outside now but so far I've seen only a couple of other people. The air is still full of noise as the military try to expose us and flush us out into the open but the streets are empty. I know there's supposed to be a curfew at night but I'm sure that's not the only reason why there's no-one around. Being out in the open is too dangerous. Those few people I have seen – the occasional solitary figure that creeps carefully through the shadows like me – I have kept away from. I don't want to risk making contact with anyone. Will they be like me? Perhaps they will but I can't afford to take any chances. They could be like the rest of them. I'll kill again if I have to but I'm not looking for trouble. Finding Ellis is more important. Tonight it feels as if the 'normal' part of the population have been driven into hiding in fear of us.

I think I'm probably about halfway between my flat and Liz's sister's house now. I had planned to walk all night but I think it will be sensible to stop and take cover soon. There are helicopters over the city again now and I feel exposed. Instinct tells me it'll soon be too much of a risk to be out alone in the darkness with the military swarming through the streets and the skies. If I thought it was safe to keep going I would. I'll take this opportunity to rest for a while and eat.

I can't stop thinking about Ellis. My poor little girl is stuck in the middle of a group of people who will turn against her at any time and without any warning. She's in danger and there's nothing I can do to help her. It might already be too late but I can't allow myself to think like that. I've consciously tried to block them from my mind but I find myself thinking about Lizzie, Edward and Josh again. Remembering them fills me with an overpowering sadness and remorse. I wonder if they might eventually change too? Could whatever has changed within me be buried somewhere inside them also? I'd like to believe it could but I don't hold out much hope. The government information I read earlier (if any of it was correct) said that just a small percentage of the population were likely to be affected. I sensed a difference between Ellis and the others too. She and I are alike. We're different from them, I can feel it. I have to accept that the rest of my family are lost.

I'm heading out of the city now. I look back over my shoulder and see that although there are still lights on in many buildings, there are also huge swathes of town which are bathed in darkness. The power must be down. It's inevitable, I suppose. This 'change' (whatever it is) might only be affecting a minority, but it's repercussions are being felt everywhere. It's tearing society apart as quickly as it destroyed my family.

I turn a corner and walk straight into another body coming the other way, the first person I've come across for some time. I immediately tense myself, ready for the kill. I push the dark figure back and clench my fists ready to strike. I stare through the darkness into the other person's face and . . . and it's okay. There is no anger, no hate and no threat. The mutual unspoken feeling of relief is immense. This person is like me and we both know that neither of us has anything to fear from the other.

'You okay?' I ask, keeping my voice low.

The other person nods and walks on.

I can hear engines in the distance. The military are still moving through the dark city behind me and they are closer now. There are more helicopters crawling through the sky too. I can see four of them hovering ominously, sweeping over the streets and occasionally illuminating the ground below them with impossibly bright spotlights. It's definitely time to get under cover.

I cross over a low stone bridge which spans a silent railway track. Ahead of me is the dark silhouette of a huge factory or ware-house and, on the other side of the road, a building site. As I get closer I see that it's the beginnings of a new housing estate. There are a few houses almost completed just off the main road and they are surrounded by the shells of other partially constructed build-ings. The half-built walls and wooden frames jutting up into the air make it hard to tell whether the houses are going up or coming down. It's a silent and desolate place and it seems a sensible place to stop and shelter for a while.

The paving slabs and tarmac beneath my feet give way to gravel and dirt. I follow the muddy and uneven route deeper into the centre of the building site and find myself walking along a row of six homes of varying shapes, sizes and degrees of construction. The ground has been so badly churned by machinery here that it takes me a while to realise that I'm actually walking through the future back gardens of these buildings, not across the front. I wonder whether any of these houses will ever be finished now? The three furthest from me appear to be the most complete and I head towards them. Their windows and doors are covered with grey metal grilles. All except the middle one of the three. The grille which covered the space where its back door was intended to go has been prised off. It's lying on the ground in a puddle of mud, buckled and useless. I'm standing in front of the doorway now, looking inside. Has someone been here? I realise that there could still be people inside but I need to stop. Should I go in? Is it safe? Sensing that nowhere's safe any more I climb the step and cau-tiously enter the building. If there is anyone in there and they're not like me I'll kill them.

Footsteps in the darkness. Sudden movement.

I try to move back but before I can react a figure is on top of me. My legs are kicked out from under me and I'm sent flying back across the hard concrete floor. I can't see anything. I try to kick and punch myself free and stand up but before I can move I'm knocked back down again. I can feel someone pressing down on my ankles and someone else has their hands on my shoulders, keeping me flat on the ground. There's a third person in here. I can see their shadow moving past the doorway.

'Think he's safe?' someone asks. They switch on a torch and the unexpected brightness burns my eyes.

'Turn it off,' I hear another one of them say in a loud, relieved whisper. 'He's all right.'

As quickly as the hands grabbed hold of me they now let go. I shuffle back across the floor, putting as much distance as I can between me and whoever else is in here. The light in the half-finished house is limited and I'm struggling to see anything. Some-one's moving just ahead of me. I know there are at least three people in here but are there any more? The torch is switched on again.

'Take it easy, mate,' one of them says. 'We're not going to hurt you.'

I don't know if I believe him. I don't know if I believe anyone any more.

The figure holding the torch shines the light into their own face. It's a man, perhaps mid-to-late twenties. I know instantly that he's like me and that I'm safe with him. And if this man is no threat then the people who are with him are no threat either.

'What's your name?' he asks.

'Danny,' I tell him, 'Danny McCoyne.'

'Been like this for long, love?' asks a woman's voice.

'What?' I mumble back.

'Been long since it happened?' she asks, rephrasing her question. I assume she's talking about what happened at home when I killed Harry and lost my family.

'Few hours,' I mumble, my throat dry. 'Not sure . . .'

'I'm Patrick,' the man holding the torch says, holding out his hand. I'm not sure whether he wants me to shake it or whether he's going to pull me up. I reach out and he helps me to stand. 'Happened to me three days ago,' he continues. 'Same for Nancy here. That's Craig,' he says, pointing the torch at the third person across the room. 'Yesterday afternoon, wasn't it, Craig?'

'Just after dinner,' Craig answers. Patrick shines the torch at him but it only illuminates a small part of a huge expanse of belly. Craig is immense.

'So what happened?' Nancy asks. 'Anyone close?'

'My partner's dad,' I explain, feeling some sadness but no remorse or guilt over what I've done. 'He just turned on me. Thought he was going to kill me so I . . .'

'Had to get him first?' she interrupts, finishing my sentence for me. My eyes are getting used to the darkness in the house now. I can see Nancy nodding and I immediately know that she completely understands what I had to do and why I had to do it, even if I'm still not sure myself. 'Everything will start to make more sense soon,' she tells me. 'I was just the same when it happened to me. Hated myself for doing it but I didn't have any choice. I'd been with John for almost thirty years and we'd hardly spent a day apart in all that time. It was just like someone had flicked a switch. I knew I had to do it.'

This is in danger of turning into a comedy of errors. Have they all killed? I ask the question without realising I'm speaking out loud.

'Suppose it just depends where you are when it happens,' Patrick says. 'Craig hasn't killed anyone yet, which is a surprise when you look at the size of the bugger!'

Nancy takes up Craig's story.

'Tried though, didn't you, love,' she sighs. In the circle of torchlight I see him nod. 'Bunch of them had you cornered at work, didn't they?'

'I was picking orders in the warehouse with four of them,' the giant of a man explains in a surprisingly soft voice. 'Didn't know what was happening. I started on one of them but there were too many. They shut me in one of the offices but I managed to get out of a window. All I could do was run.'

This conversation is bizarre and uncomfortably surreal. It only becomes believable again when I remember the fact that I've killed twice today. How could that be? Christ, until this morning I hadn't even hit anyone in temper, let alone killed them. Patrick passes me a bottle of water which I drink from thirstily.

'What about you?' I ask him.

'I killed,' he answers. 'Don't know who the guy was, I just had to do it like the rest of you. He was just stood there staring at me as I was getting into the car . . .'

'. . . and?'

'And I mowed him down. Started the engine, chased him down the street and I mowed him down. Pretty much wrote the car off too. Just kept driving along with him under the wheels. I didn't know what else to do. Tried to go back home but when I got there I saw that my girl was just like the rest of them and . . .'

'. . . and you know the rest of the story,' Craig grumbles. 'You just have to do it, don't you?'

'It feels like second nature,' Patrick says quietly. 'It's instinctive. It's animal instinct.'

The room falls silent.

'So what happens now?' I ask.

'Who knows,' Nancy answers. 'My guess is we'll just keep killing each other until either we're all gone or they are. Crazy, isn't it?'

It's hard to get my head round the fact that this woman (who looks like any other average wife / mother / daughter / sister / aunt) is talking so matter-of-factly about killing. In the days since she's changed she seems to have relinquished every aspect of her former life and is now prepared to kill to stay alive herself. At moments like this it all seems beyond belief. Nancy looks more likely to bake you a cake than kill you. I shake my head in bewilderment as Craig gets up and drags a wooden board across the open doorway, blocking out the last shards of light coming in from outside.

35

'So how much of it have you worked out then?' Patrick asks. We're both upstairs in what was probably destined to be the master bedroom of the half-finished house, sitting with our backs to the recently plastered wall. The sky has cleared now and the moon is providing limited but welcome illumination through the grille over the window. I'm tired and I don't want to talk but I can't avoid answering his question.

'Haven't got a bloody clue what's going on,' I answer honestly. 'This is as close as I've managed to get,' I say as I take the folded-up booklet from my bag and pass it to him. He scans the pages by the light of his torch and smiles wryly to himself.

'Good stuff, this!' he laughs sarcastically.

'Took it from a house I hid in,' I tell him. 'Doesn't say much.'

'When did you last get anything from the government that did?'

He shuts the booklet and throws it down onto the bare floor-boards.

'It's not like there's anyone you can ask about it, is there?' I say. 'I still don't know if anyone really knows what's happening.'

'Someone knows,' he mutters, 'they must do. You can bet that from the second the first person changed, some government depart-ment somewhere has been analysing us and cutting up people like you and me and . . .'

'Cutting up people?'

'I'm exaggerating,' he continues, 'but you know what I'm saying, don't you? They'll have had a team of top scientists sitting in some lab somewhere working out what's happened to us. They'll be working on a cure.'

'You reckon?'

He shrugs his shoulders.

'Maybe. Whatever happens they'll be trying to find a way of stopping us doing what we do.'

I know he's right. We're a threat to them. Far more of a threat than any enemy they might have battled with previously.

'I don't want to be cured,' I say, surprising even myself with my admission. 'I want to stay like this. I don't want to go back to being one of them.'

Patrick nods and switches off his torch. In the darkness I find myself thinking about Ellis again. I know that it's only a matter of time before she changes if she hasn't already. I've tried to convince myself that she'll be all right but I know that as long as she's with the others she's in danger. The hardest thing to come to terms with today – harder even than everything I've lost – is the fact that Lizzie, the person who carried my little girl and who has provided her with more safety and security than anyone else, is now the one who poses the biggest threat to her. The pain I feel when I think about Ellis tonight is indescribable. Maybe I should try and get to her now. Poor little thing doesn't know what's going to happen. She hasn't got a clue . . .

'Don't say a lot, do you?' Patrick pushes. He's beginning to get on my nerves but I sense that he has a need to talk. He's as nervous, scared and confused as I am so I don't retaliate.

'Not much to say, is there?' I grunt back.

'So who are you thinking about?'

Very perceptive. I pause but then decide to answer him. Maybe it will help.

'My little girl. She's like us.'

'Why isn't she with you?'

'Because of her mother. I was in the house with the whole family when it happened. I knew that Ellis was like me and I tried to get her but . . .'

'But what?'

'Lizzie got to her before me. Smacked me around the face with a bloody metal pipe. Next thing I knew she'd gone and taken all the kids with her.'

Patrick shakes his head.

'Too bad,' he mumbles. 'Hurts when you lose them, doesn't it?'

I nod, but I don't know if he notices my response.

'What about you?' I ask. 'You said something earlier about your partner . . .'

He doesn't answer for a few long seconds.

'Like I said, I managed to get back home after it happened. You know almost before you see them that they haven't changed, don't you? I did what I had to do.'

I don't know what he means by that. Did he kill her? I quickly decide that it's probably not a good idea to ask. For a moment I think that's the end of the conversation but then Patrick speaks again.

'Got it all wrong, didn't they?' he says.

'What?'

'The papers and the TV and all that,' he explains, 'made us out to be the villains of the piece, didn't they?'

'To them we are.'

'Made it out to be us that hated them . . .'

'I never hated anyone,' I tell him, 'at least not like they said on the news.'

In the moonlight I watch as Patrick nods knowingly. He's not stupid. He's spent the last three days thinking about what I've only had a few hours to try and understand.

'Know what I think?'

'What?' I reply, yawning.

'They called us the Haters, because from their perspective all we're doing is attacking and killing. That's how it looked to me before I changed. You agree?'

'Suppose.'

'But the fact of the matter is that everybody hates. They're just as bad as we are. They want us dead as much as we want to get rid of them. You can feel the hate coming off them, can't you? Even if they're not capable of showing it like we are or dealing with it like we do, they want us dead. So all we're doing is protecting our-selves. You just know that you have to do it, don't you? You have to kill them before they get to you.'

'We're as bad as each other then,' I suggest.

'Maybe. Like I said everybody hates, we're just better at dealing with it than they are. We have to look after ourselves and if it means destroying them, then that's what we have to do.'

'Problem is they feel exactly the same . . .'

'I know. But they're not as physical or aggressive as we are and that's where we have the advantage. They don't move quickly enough. They'll pay the price eventually.'

'So what is it that's changed?' I ask. 'And why now? Why has this happened to some of us and not others? Why has it happened at all?'

'Now that's the big question, isn't it? That's the one I can't work out the answer to, and you can bet we won't find any clues in your bloody government brochure either.'

'But what do you think's caused it?'

'Don't know. I've come up with about a hundred possible explanations so far,' he chuckles, 'but they're all bullshit!'

'Is it a disease? Have we caught something?'

He shakes his head.

'Maybe we have. The way I look at it there's two possible explanations. Either it is a virus or something like that, or maybe something has happened to everyone. People like you and me have been affected by it, the rest of them haven't changed at all.'

'Something like what?'

'I don't know . . . maybe someone put something in the water? Perhaps the planet's drifted through a cloud of bloody space gas or something! Maybe it's just evolution? Nature taking its course . . .'

Patrick chuckles to himself again. The room then becomes silent and the quiet gives me chance to consider what he's just said. He could be right. If this was a virus or disease, surely more people would have been directly affected? Everything is so screwed up tonight that all of his disjointed and unsubstantiated theories sound plausible.

'So how many people like us do you think there are?' I ask, knowing that he can't do anything other than guess at the answer.

'No idea,' he replies. 'Last thing I remember hearing they were talking about a small minority of people, and that's what it says in your booklet here. But I think it's bigger than anyone's letting on. Chances are no-one knows how big it is.'

'And how widespread? Surely this can't just be happening here?'

'It spread up and down the country quickly enough, didn't it? So if one country's been affected . . .'

'. . . then why not everywhere else?'

'Exactly.'

'So where does it end?'

More silence.

'Don't know. Don't even know if I want to think about it. We have to keep fighting to stay alive, and you can bet they're going to be doing exactly the same thing. So we can only keep running and keep killing,' he replies, 'because if we don't get them, they'll get us.'

36

Patrick has finally shut up. I lie on the cold floor and try to sleep and rest my brain and my body. I can't stop thinking about Ellis. In the morning, I decide, I'll carry on towards Liz's sister's house and look for her there. I just pray that nothing happens before I reach her.

In the morning I might risk taking a car for speed. I feel strong and calm and I'm prepared to walk the rest of the way but I'll be quicker driving, albeit much more exposed and vulnerable. It doesn't seem to matter now. What I'm doing feels so right. The life I've left behind seems more alien and unnatural with each passing minute. I wouldn't go back to it now, even if I had the choice. I just wish that Lizzie, Edward and Josh could be like Ellis and me.

There's more noise outside. It's early in the morning – two or three o'clock I think – and there's a constant stream of sound coming from the middle of town. I can hear more trucks and helicopters. More patrols flushing people out. Whatever happens tomorrow I know I'll have to leave here. I don't want to stay in one place for too long. I'll keep moving until I find Ellis and then, when I've got her back, we'll run together. We'll find somewhere safe where there are more people like us, well away from those that hate us. And if we can't find anywhere safe then we'll kill and destroy as many of them as we have to. It's like the man said, we have to kill them before they kill us.

I'll sleep now and make my move at first light.

SATURDAY

37

'Get out!' a terrified voice screams over a God-awful noise. 'For Christ's sake, get out of here!'

I sit up quickly. My body aches from sleeping on the bare floorboards. The half-built house is filled with a deafening thumping sound. I run to the window and push my face against the grey metal grille, desperate to see outside. There's a helicopter hovering nearby. It's not directly over the building site but it's close enough and I know that it's people like us they're looking for. I look around and see that I'm alone. Patrick's gone but his stuff is still here.

Shit. There's a truck at the end of the gravel track and soldiers are already piling out of the back of it and running towards these houses. I have to move. I grab my bag and head for the door. I can hear a loudhailer outside, someone shouting a warning about standing still and not moving and . . . gunfire. I run back to the window and look down again and now I can see Craig face down in a puddle of mud, a rifle-wielding soldier standing over his fallen bulk with his still smoking gun aimed at the back of his head. I can see Patrick and Nancy too, both trying to get away. More troops swarm around them quickly, cutting off their escape route as another truck arrives.

I have to get away from here. Maybe I could get up into the loft space and hide or should I just try and make a run for it? Is it too high to jump down from one of the windows up here? I can't allow myself to get caught. I have to get out of here and get Ellis. Now I can hear footsteps downstairs. Loud, heavy, clunking footsteps. Christ, they probably already know I'm up here. I run towards one of the smaller back rooms and meet a masked soldier coming the other way. I try to push past him but the fucker punches me in the face and before I can react I'm flat on my back looking up at the ceiling. I try to stand up but rough hands grab my arms and I'm dragged downstairs. There's no point fighting, I think, as I try not to panic. My only option now is to wait until I'm outside and then try to run. But then I think of that poor bastard Craig, face down, riddled with bullets. Cooperate with them I decide, despite the fact that every single nerve, sinew and fibre of my body wants to fight these animals and destroy them.

I'm dragged through the hallway and kitchen and then out of the building. They shove me towards the truck where Nancy and Patrick stand trembling. I trip and fall to my knees in the mud close to Patrick's feet.

'Get up!' one of the soldiers screams in my ear and a hand grabs me by the scruff of my neck and pulls me up. Patrick looks at me. I see desperation, terror and frustration in his frightened eyes.

What now? I think to myself. Come on, if you're going to kill me just do it. Let's get it over with. There are guns pointed at us, but surely they'd have shot us by now if they were going to? I look up at the nearest soldier. A dark visor obscures his eyes but I can sense the hate coming off him like the stench of decay. Two more uniformed figures emerge from the front of the first truck and walk towards us. One of them is carrying one of the flat computers I've seen them using before. The other has a smaller electronic device held in one hand. I can't see what it is. They move quickly. One of them shoves me back against the side of the truck while the other holds the small device up to my throat. There's a split-second hiss of air then I feel a sudden, stinging pain in the side of my neck like an insect bite. They let me go and turn their attention to Patrick then Nancy, doing exactly the same to both of them. Bizarrely they then use the machine on Craig's dead body.

We stand in a line at the side of the truck, silent and not daring to move. The soldiers connect the handheld device to their computer and study the screen.

'Well?' asks one of the other troops from a short distance away.

'All of them,' the computer operator replies.

'Any IDs?'

'Just one, Patrick Crilley,' he says, pointing at him. Patrick looks anxiously from side to side. 'Can't match the others.'

The first soldier turns away and makes a dismissive hand signal to the other troops who still surround us with their guns raised. I bite my lip and force myself not to react as one of them grabs my shoulder and pushes me towards the back of the truck.

'In,' he grunts. I stand my ground and stare into his visor. Two more of them come at me from the side and, grabbing a leg each, they lift me up and shove me through a grubby tarpaulin cover and into the truck. I land flat on my face in the darkness and, before I can move, Patrick and Nancy land heavily on top of me. My face is pressed hard against the dirty floor and I'm shoved further down as the other two struggle to disentangle themselves from each other.

'You're all right,' a voice that I don't recognise whispers from close to where I've fallen. 'You're with friends here.'

Whoever's on top of me manages to drag themselves up onto their feet and I'm finally able to get up myself. I try and stand but the engine of the truck is started and the sudden lurching movement as it pulls away causes me to fall again. Someone helps me up and, for the first time, I'm able to look around. I count the dark shapes of seventeen other people in here including Patrick and Nancy. The light is poor but I know immediately that they're all like me. Seventeen men, women and children just like me.

38

We've been driving for what feels like hours but I know it hasn't been anywhere near that long. We paused another five (might have been six) times to pick up more people but it's been a while since we last stopped. There are now twenty-eight of us in here, I think. It's a relief to be with so many people like me but space is limited and it's hot and bloody uncomfortable in here. I assume the truck is full now, so where the hell are they taking us? My home and family and everything else that's gone seems a million miles away. I know that the distance between me and Ellis is increasing with every minute I spend trapped in this bloody truck.

The tarpaulin cover over our heads blocks out most of the light so it's difficult to see much in here. I've managed to drag myself over to one side of the vehicle and someone nearby has been able to lift up a small flap of material. I can't see very much through the gap, just the edge of the road rushing by. We've not slowed to take any turnings for some time. We must be on a major road and it must be virtually empty. I'm practically blind and I can't hear anything over the clattering engine of the truck and the rumble of the wheels on the tarmac. The world feels alien and desolate and the disorientation of the journey makes it a hundred times worse.

The few faces I can make out nearest to me appear beaten, empty and expressionless. No-one understands what's happened to them or why. People are too frightened and confused to talk and so remain silent and subdued. There's no conversation, just the odd whispered word. I wish there was some distraction. Without anything else to occupy my mind all I can do is remember Ellis and also think about what might be waiting for me at the end of this journey. Where are we being taken, and what's going to happen when we get there? Someone near the back makes a half-hearted attempt to open the back of the truck. For a few seconds an escape seems possible until we find that the tarpaulin has been secured from outside. We're trapped in here.

There's a girl sitting next to me who is gradually becoming more and more agitated. I've consciously tried not to stare at anyone in the semi-darkness but I've seen enough to know that she's young and pretty although her face is tired and grubby and is streaked with tears. She's in her late teens I think, maybe older. She's leaning against me and I can feel her body shaking. She's been sobbing for some time. Christ, I'm scared, how the hell must she be feeling? She looks up at me and makes eye contact for the first time.

'I feel sick,' she whimpers. 'I think I'm going to be ill.' I'm no good at dealing with vomit. Please don't throw up, I think to myself.

'Take deep breaths,' I suggest, 'it's probably just nerves. Try and take some deep breaths.'

'It's not nerves,' she says, 'I get travel sick.'

Great. Without thinking I hold her arm and start to rub her back with my other hand. It's more of a comfort for me than anything else.

'What's your name?' I ask, hoping that I might be able to distract her and take her mind off how ill she's feeling.

'Karin,' she replies.

And now I'm stuck for something to say. What can I talk to her about? If she's anything like me she'll have found she's suddenly become a homeless, family-less and friend-less killer. There's no point trying to make small talk. Bloody idiot, I wish I hadn't said any-thing.

'Do you think we're going to be in here much longer?' she asks, her breathing suddenly shallow.

'No idea,' I answer truthfully.

'Where are they taking us?'

'Don't know. Look, the best thing you can do is try and take your mind off it. Just find something else to concentrate on and . . .'

It's too late, she's beginning to heave. She grabs my hand as she starts to convulse. I try and turn her around so she can be sick out through the small gap in the tarpaulin but there's not enough space and not enough time. She throws up, splattering the inside of the truck and my boots and trousers with puke.

'Sorry,' she moans as the smell hits me. I'm struggling to control my own stomach now. I can taste bile in the back of my throat and

I can hear other people gagging and groaning in disgust all around me.

'Doesn't matter,' I mumble. The inside of the truck, which was already hot and musty because of the sheer number of people trapped inside it, now stinks. It's impossible to escape the smell but I have to try and do something otherwise I'll shortly be adding to the stench myself. I stand up, holding onto the side of the truck for support and, now that I'm upright, I notice a small rip in the tarpaulin at my eye level. I look closer and see that it's a seam which has begun to come undone. I push my fingers into the gap and try to open out my hand. As I stretch my fingers the stitching holding the material together frays and comes apart. Finally some welcome daylight and much needed cool, fresh air is able to flood into the truck. Not giving a damn about the consequences I shove both hands into the rip and pull as hard as I can in either direction. The gap increases in size to about half a metre and I can hear the relief of the people around me.

'Can you see where we are?' a voice asks from somewhere on the other side of the truck. All I can see are trees at the side of the road as we rush past.

'Haven't got a clue,' I answer. 'Can't see much.'

'You can see more than me,' the voice snaps, 'keep looking.'

I push my head right out through the canopy and try to look up towards the front of the truck. We're on a motorway, I think. The long and relatively featureless road gradually curves away to the left and, for the first time, I see that we're not travelling alone. There's another truck in front. Hold on, there's more than one. It's difficult to be sure, but I think I can see at least another five vehicles ahead of us, all trucks of a similar size to this one, equally spaced from each other. Taking care not to slip in the gross puddle at my feet I shuffle around so that I can look behind us. I count at least as many trucks again following, probably more.

'Well?' the voice asks as I pull my head back inside.

'Can't see where we are,' I reply, loud enough for everyone to hear, 'but we're not on our own.'

'What?'

'There are loads of trucks like this,' I tell them, 'at least ten that I can see.'

'So where are they taking us?' another frightened voice asks, not really expecting an answer. 'What are they going to do with us?'

'Don't know,' I hear Patrick reply in his familiar resigned tone, 'but you can bet it's going to be fucking awful, whatever it is.'

I stick my head back out of the side of the truck again to escape the stink of vomit and the nervous, frightened conversations which Patrick's accurate but insensitive comments have just started.

39

We finally slow down and the truck makes an unexpected swinging turn to the left. It's a sharp bend, too severe to be a normal motorway exit. The road we're travelling along becomes rough and uneven and continues to twist and turn for what feels like another mile or two further. Then, without any warning, the journey's over. We've stopped. My stomach churns with nerves again as the truck comes to a sudden halt and its engine is silenced. It's pouring with rain outside and the clattering noise on the roof above my head is deafening.

'Where are we now?' someone asks nervously. I dutifully shove my head back out through the tear in the tarpaulin and quickly pull it in again when I see soldiers approaching on foot. I wait until they've passed before cautiously peering back out. The truck and the ten or so other vehicles which have travelled in convoy with us have stopped in a line along a narrow road which runs along the edge of what looks like a dense forest. I can't see where the track goes from here. I don't want to risk leaving myself exposed like this for any longer than necessary and I close up the gap in the heavy canvas cover. I'm sure we'll be seeing where we are soon enough.

'There's not much to see,' I tell them all unhelpfully as I turn back round and crouch down again, 'just trees on that side.' The rain is torrential and I have to shout to make myself heard. The sound of the water hitting the tight cover above us is relentless. The noise combines with the lack of any strong light to increase my disorientation. I can't stand this. I wonder again whether I should just take my chances and make a run for it? What have I got to lose when I've already lost just about everything? I don't know what other options I have left. Things look increasingly bleak. Do I just sit here and wait for whatever they have planned for us to happen or do I take control of my destiny now and try to escape? The little of the forest I've been able to see so far looks pretty deep and uninviting. We seem to be right out in the middle of nowhere and there's no way they'd be able to follow me into the trees in these trucks. They'll either shoot me in the back as I'm running or I'll manage to get away. It has to be worth taking a chance. My mind starts to fill with images of getting back home and finding Ellis again and the decision is made. First chance I get I'll go for it. Christ knows where I'll run to, but anywhere will be better than here. Do I tell any of the others what I'm planning? Do I stand more chance running with them or on my own? My instincts tell me to leave them and look after myself, but what about the rest of them? What about Karin and Nancy and Patrick? Surely the more people who run, the better our chances are of getting away . . . ?

My stupid plans come crashing down around me as the flap at the back of the vehicle is thrown open by two rain-soaked soldiers. One of them ties the tarpaulin up, the other points the rifle into the truck. The reality of what's happening suddenly hits home again now that I'm back looking down the barrel of another gun. The plans I'd been seriously considering seconds earlier now seem stupid. More than ever I want to fight but to run now would be suicidal.

'Out!' the soldier with the rifle barks at us. 'Get out now!'

Those nearest the back of the truck immediately begin to climb out. It's a drop of several feet down to the muddy track and more than one person loses their footing and falls. Poor bastards, they've only been outside for seconds and they're already cold and soaked. One of the men in here with me – a young, slim man with long, dark hair – rushes one of the soldiers as soon as he hits the ground. Three more troopers appear from nowhere and pull him away from their colleague. Two of them throw him down and push him face first into the grass at the side of the road. The third soldier lifts a pistol and puts a bullet in the back of his head. The frenzied attack and clinical response is over in seconds and the corpse is dragged away. There are sobs and wails of fear and disbelief from the people already outside.

I'm one of the last to leave the truck. I climb out backwards and slip but somehow manage to stay upright when I jump down. The others have been lined up in single file on the verge between the trees and the trucks. One of the soldiers shoves me towards the line. I stand my ground for a second and stare at the trooper. His eyes are hidden and I can see my bruised face reflected in his opaque visor. I should kill him now, I think to myself. And I know I could do it too. I could snap his neck with my bare hands. This piece of shit deserves nothing more than a violent, painful and very bloody death for his part in what's happening to us. But then I look past him and see more of them lumping away the lifeless body of the man they've just shot in the head. They leave him lying in full view, unceremoniously dumped on the other side of the road, and I reluctantly take my place in the queue.

From where I'd been standing I'd only been able to see the people who'd travelled in the same truck as me. Now that I've moved I can see that the people from the other vehicles have been dragged out into the open too. The queue of people ahead of me stretches away into the distance. I line up behind Karin, the girl who was sick earlier.

'You okay?' I whisper. I glance over at the nearest soldiers but they don't react and I risk trying to speak to her again. 'Karin, are you okay?' She turns around momentarily and nods her head but doesn't speak. Her face is pale and her teeth are chattering with the cold. The rain is coming down so hard on us now that it hurts. I've only been outside for a couple of minutes and I'm already soaked to the skin. At least I've got a few layers of clothes on. Up ahead of me I can see people who are only wearing T-shirts. Some are still in their pyjamas. One old guy is just wearing a dressing gown. Poor bastards must have been taken in the night while they were sleeping. Couldn't they have let them change or given them something warmer to wear? It shows just how deep-rooted their hate of us really is and it's suddenly more apparent than ever that the throwaway comment Patrick made in the back of the truck was right. Whatever's waiting for us here is going to be fucking awful. At best they've brought us here to keep us isolated and separate from them. And the worst-case scenario? I know there's a very high probability that we're here to be destroyed. They can try and kill me but when the time comes I'll go out fighting. I owe it to Ellis to take out as many of them as I can.

Christ, what about Ellis?! How could I be so stupid? I've been so wrapped up in what's happening to me that I haven't stopped to consider the possibility that my little girl might have been brought here too. What if she changed like me and was picked up by one of the patrols? I know the chance of finding her here is slim but I have to try. I can see some children in the line up ahead but even from this distance I know that my daughter isn't one of them. I turn around and try to look behind me. Bloody hell, this queue of people seems to go on for ever. I can't see the end of it. I've stepped right out of line now but I don't care. Finding Ellis is more important than my own safety. I start to move further down the queue but stop when a hand grabs my shoulder and yanks me back into position. I turn round expecting to be facing a guard but it's Karin.

'Don't be stupid,' she whispers, looking around anxiously. 'Please, they'll kill you just as soon as look at you.'

I nod but say nothing. I know she's right. I return to my original place in the queue and try and force myself to accept the reality of the situation. I was taken hours after Liz took Ellis from me and in a completely different part of town from where I think they would have gone. The chances of her being here are slight. And if we're taken on from here to some other central location, I think, then there will probably be more chance of me finding her there.

I have to try and stay in control and wait for the right moment but it's difficult. I want to run and fight and destroy the soldiers surrounding us. I need to move and take action but I can't. Standing here and waiting like this is unbearable. These conditions are deceptively harsh. I'm so wet that my clothes feel heavy and their waterlogged weight is beginning to drag me down. We are all drenched with rain and numb with cold and all we can do is stand still and wait.

Sudden activity again. It's been some time but I have no idea how long has passed since we were thrown out of the trucks. I'm still managing to stay on my feet but I've seen a handful of people fall further along the queue. No-one dares move to help them. Each of us knows that to risk moving is to risk taking a bullet from the scum surrounding us. There are hundreds of people in this queue and soldiers continue to patrol the line constantly, rifles armed and primed and ready to fire. I have to concentrate hard to stop myself from breaking ranks and killing them. It's torture. Is this how they're planning to get rid of us all? Just leave us standing here in the middle of nowhere until the last one falls?

I heard a burst of radio static a few moments ago. Around half the soldiers have suddenly returned to their vehicles leaving the other half to hold their positions at the side of the queue, their weapons constantly trained on us. Now the engines of the trucks have been started again and the vehicles are moving away in convoy. They power past us at speed, showering us with mud and water from potholes and puddles in the road.

For the first time I can clearly see what's on the other side of the track.

Through the persistent heavy rain I can see an enormous expanse of land, empty but for a single grey-white building right in the centre. It looks like a factory, or maybe some kind of agricultural storage site or warehouse. There are two huge silos to the left and the whole scene looks strangely dilapidated and untidy. An empty tarmac track runs from the front of the building across the field to the road on which we're queuing. And now I can also see that this queue stretches all the way along the road up virtually as far as the entrance to the field. Christ, there must be thousands of us here.

There's activity all around the building in the distance. From here it's not possible to see what's happening clearly. I can see soldiers and other dark-suited figures moving constantly. Some are removing equipment from the building, others are taking things in. I have no idea what any of it is. I don't think I want to know.

Just ahead of me the sudden activity has caused someone's nerve to break. There's panic in the queue and for a second I'm struggling to see who it is and what's happening. Looks like someone has broken rank and jumped one of the soldiers. Do I use this distraction as cover and try and get away myself? Other people are thinking the same thing. At least two people are already running into the trees. Now five, six, seven . . . maybe as many as ten more figures are sprinting into the forest. I have to move now if I'm ever going to do it. The soldiers nearest to me are distracted and if I'm fast I can . . .

Fuckers. The break-out is over as quickly as it started. Two soldiers step forward and unload their automatic weapons into the trees. The people running are brought down without warning – shot in the back and killed. Many more people who were still standing in line in the queue up ahead have been caught in the cross-fire and are dead too. I know that the same thing will happen to me if I try anything.

The soldiers regroup and retake their positions. One of them makes a call on their radio and then, after a short delay, a van appears from alongside the building up ahead and drives out towards the road. It stops on the other side of the track at the point where the shooting took place. People standing in the queue are forced at gunpoint to gather the bodies of the dead and load them into the van. Helplessly I watch as two sobbing women are made to drag the corpses out of the forest and carry them across the road. An older man and a teenage girl are sent down to collect the body of the man from my truck who was shot in the head earlier.

40

The torrential rain has continued and shows no signs of stopping. The grey clouds overhead are darker than ever and the light is fading quickly. Don't think I can stay standing like this for much longer. I can't feel my feet or my hands any more. The skin on my face is raw and I'm numb with cold. I haven't had anything to drink all day but my bladder feels full and the pain is excruciating.

I'm scared. Every time one of the soldiers near to me moves I catch my breath, not because I'm afraid of them, but because inside I'm screaming with frustration, desperate to fight and to kill the evil scum that is holding us captive here. But I know that I can't. There are too many of them and they are too heavily armed. If I dared show my intentions they would destroy me in seconds. I can't let that happen but it's getting harder and harder to keep these emotions under control. I know that elsewhere along the line other people have been unable to hold back and have paid for it with their lives. Just a few minutes ago I heard a single scream of rage followed by a hail of bullets in the gloom behind me. The silence around us now is somehow even more frightening than the sounds of fighting and death which preceded it.

As the day has dragged on it has become impossible to see either end of the line. In the low light I can only see as far as about thirty people ahead of me and a similar number behind. I'm sure that the queue has grown hundreds of people longer. Twice in the last hour or so convoys of empty trucks have driven past us. Logic says they've brought more people here and they're now back out on the streets again looking for others.

The girl in front of me is swaying on her feet again. I can't let her fall. I shuffle forward slightly and put my hand out to steady her.

'Come on,' I hiss under my breath, 'not now. Try to hold on . . .' I don't even know if she can hear me over the driving rain.

Something's happening up ahead. I can't see anything but I can definitely hear something. I peer into the gloom, desperate to try and see what's going on. Are people finally starting to move? For a few seconds longer I'm unsure but then an unexpected ripple of movement works its way along the line to a point where I can finally see what's happening. We're starting to shuffle forward. A sudden wave of awkward, stumbling movement reaches me and for the first time in hours I start to walk. My legs are agonisingly stiff and every step takes a massive amount of effort and coordination. For a moment I stupidly feel relieved when the pain in my aching legs begins to fade slightly, but then I start to think about what we might be walking towards and the panic returns. I know that making a run for it is out of the question for now. Just putting one foot in front of the other is difficult enough. I don't have the strength or the energy to be able to move any faster.

The soldiers continue to march alongside us, keeping their distance most of the time but occasionally hitting and shoving those of us who move too slowly or who stumble out of line. Just ahead another one of the men who travelled in the same truck as me drops to the ground. He's old and tired and he lies on the gravel track sobbing. I keep walking – I have no choice – and I listen as one of the soldiers yells at him to get back to his feet and keep moving. I wish I could do something to help. I daren't look round. I hear a single gunshot close behind me and I know that his suffering is over. My fury now feels harder than ever to contain. Despite my exhaustion the urge to turn on these soldiers and fight them – to kill them – is growing stronger by the minute and is almost impossible to suppress. It's only the obvious fact that any reaction would inevitably be the last thing I do that keeps me in line.

We've stopped again.

Almost as quickly as the movement began it now ends. I have no idea how far we've moved. I don't know how much closer to it I now am but I assume the people at the front of the queue have finally been led down the track towards the entrance to the building.

41

Christ it's cold.

The cloud cover has lifted slightly and, for a while at least, the rain has finally eased. The building up ahead has been illuminated by a series of bright floodlights which shine up from the ground and make it look like some bloody Gothic cathedral or fortress. Although I can see it more clearly now I still have no idea what the purpose of it is. Is it some kind of quarantine centre? None of this makes any sense. If they've brought us out here to kill us then why not just do it? Why waste all this time and manpower keeping us in line and collecting up bodies? For some of the poor bastards here in the line with me a bullet in the head would be a relief. But maybe that's what this is all about? Maybe they just want us to suffer?

After hours of inactivity we've now made three sudden stop-start shifts forward. This time I counted the number of steps I took. I think we moved about a hundred paces forward. Logic says a similar number of people have just disappeared into the building up ahead of us.

Another convoy of recently emptied trucks thunders past. Another few hundred people added to the end of the queue.

The noise of the trucks quickly fades into the distance but I can hear something else now. I can hear a plane, and the sound of its powerful engines many miles above us makes me realise just how quiet the rest of the world has become. The plane is moving with incredible speed. It must be a jet or something similar. I'm wary about making any sudden movements and looking to the sky but I can't help myself. Keeping my head as still as possible and just moving my eyes I search the heavens. And then I see it. A dark metal blur which races at a phenomenal velocity across the horizon from right to left. Even some of the soldiers have become distracted now.

Now there's a second noise. A belly-rumbling roar which I can feel through the ground beneath my feet. This noise comes from a different direction. It seems to swirl and drift in the wind before becoming louder and more definite. It's coming from behind us. I look up and watch as a single flash of light sears through the darkness miles above our heads, racing towards the jet in the distance. Was it another jet? A missile?

It can only last for a few seconds but the delay feels like for ever. I watch the white light in the sky as it hurtles towards the jet and then crashes into it, taking it out with incredible, pin-point precision. For a second a huge ball of expanding orange flame hangs in the purple sky. It has all but disappeared by the time the thundering rumble of the explosion reaches us.

We shuffle forward again.

I'm another few metres closer to the building but, for once, what's waiting in there for me is not what I'm thinking about. Instead I'm trying to work out what I've just seen happen. Regardless of who was flying the plane and who launched the missile, that was a purposeful and very definite attack and it finally gives me a little glimmer of hope. Someone, somewhere is still fighting.

42

The fear and panic in this part of the queue has reached an unbearable level. We're still moving. A relentless on-off shuffle down towards the building in the field. The nervousness of the soldiers around us seems to have increased too.

Is this a slaughterhouse? Are we going to be neutered? Have they developed a 'cure' to make us like them again? Frightened thoughts rush through my mind at a thousand miles an hour as I get closer to the building. Whatever happens in there I know I've almost reached the inevitable end of my journey. The last day has been hell but I'd go through it all again to trade places with the person at the very back of this queue. I'd give anything to put off going through those dark doors in the near distance. Despite the fact that I'm surrounded by hundreds, probably thousands of people like me, I feel completely alone. Just a few days ago everything was relatively normal and all of this would have seemed impossible. A week ago today I was sitting in the pub with my family, oblivious to everything that was about to happen to us. I think about losing Liz and Harry and Ed and Josh and it's difficult to contain my emotions. I think about Ellis and I feel like I've been stabbed through the heart.

We move along the road like we're on a chain gang. All we're missing is the shackles around our feet. Over the constant dragging sound of hundreds of exhausted footsteps I think I can hear something. There's a noise in the distance. It's quiet and indistinct but it's definitely there. A deep, far-off rumbling. Is that thunder I can hear or something else? The rain continues to lash down all around me and the low light makes it all but impossible to see what's happening away from the building.

Progress is slow but I wish it were slower still. I'm already halfway down the track which runs from the front of the building to the road and now, for the first time, I'm close enough to see some of what's happening around the entrance. The track is packed solid with people who queue up behind some kind of heavily guarded canvas-covered checkpoint. It's hard to see any detail, but from here it looks like an immigration control desk or customs point at an airport. A steady stream of people are moving past the checkpoint and are being herded into the main part of the building. They look over their shoulders in desperation as more rifle-wielding soldiers push and shove them forward. I don't even want to think about what's in there. One thing is painfully obvious – there's no apparent way out. People are going in, but as far as I can see no-one's coming out.

There's now just a few short metres between where I'm standing and the checkpoint. Up ahead there's more panic and confusion as someone breaks from the queue and attempts to run. This time they're on their own. No-one else is running with them. The lone figure which sprints away in the direction of the towering silos to my left is brought down by a hail of bullets, far more than are necessary. And bizarrely, as soon as the body is on the ground more troopers scurry across the front of the building to collect it. Instead of leaving it where it fell they pick it up and, between them, carry it inside. What the hell are they doing?

There's another noise in the distance. It has to be thunder.

We move forward again and now I'm close enough to hear some of the conversation at the checkpoint. My heart is beating at a hundred times its normal rate and my legs feel like they're about to buckle and give way beneath me. This time it has nothing to do with my tiredness, this is sheer terror. I can feel the minutes of my life ticking away and I'm devastated that it's going to end this way. Maybe I can attack, I think to myself again. Can I summon up the energy for a final strike? Am I ready to die fighting? This is my very last chance. I can see Patrick just ten people or so ahead of me. If I could somehow get his attention then just maybe together we could do something . . . Who am I kidding? I look at the nearest soldier with his rifle poised and ready to fire and I know that the odds are too one-sided to even dare consider. It would be over before I'd been able to kill even one of them.

'Name?' one of the officers at the checkpoint yells at the next person in line.

'Jason Mansell,' the man replies, his voice quiet and resigned but still carrying the slightest hint of anger and resistance.

'Date of birth?'

He answers. He's also asked for his most recent address and, while he's answering, it finally dawns on me why these bastards are treating us like shit but are also strangely concerned about our bodies. We've been stripped of all individuality and yet they still want to know who we are and where we're from. The answer is obvious – it's a bloody census. They're carrying out a bloody census of us. If they want to completely control us and wipe us out, then they have to know where every last one of us is. That was why they attempted to identify us when we were first taken at the house this morning. That's why they collect the bodies of the dead. They have to know who it is they've killed to make sure we're all accounted for. I stupidly think about giving them false information when it's my turn but I know it won't do anybody any good. As I get closer I see that they're also taking swabs from people's mouths and they're using devices to scan their eyes and palms. Christ, we must be a hell of a threat to them. They're running scared.

Another rolling roar of thunder. Storm's getting closer now. Patrick has disappeared from view and there are now just four people left ahead of me in the line. We're moving with an un-comfortable speed. People are being processed at a frantic rate which seems crazy. We've been stood out here for hours. Why start rushing now?

Three people. Wish they'd slow down.

Two people.

Now I'm next. I stand a short distance back behind two soldiers and watch as Karin is processed. I watch helplessly as one of them slams her hand down flat onto some sort of scanner as another one holds her eye open and scans her retina with another device. A few key presses on a computer keyboard and she's finished and shoved towards the dark opening to the building. There are solid lines of guards on either side. It's clear that once you're past this check-point there's nowhere else to go but inside.

'Name?' the officer at the desk shouts as I'm pushed forward.

'Danny McCoyne,' I answer. I glance to my left and see that there's a rifle pointing at my head. Just do what you're told, I think to myself, just do what you're told.

'Short for Daniel?'

I nod.

216

'Answer!'

'Yes,' I mumble.

He asks my date of birth and my most recent address and I tell him. My right hand is then grabbed and scanned. Another trooper reaches up and with rough, clumsy fingers prises open my eyelid and uses the device on me. It has a bright light which I wasn't expecting. It blinds me temporarily.

'Send him through,' I hear the officer order and I'm pushed forward into the darkness. They're definitely speeding things up now. There are too many of us being sent through too quickly. I stumble and trip towards the back of a bottleneck which is quickly forming. Behind me I hear the next person being processed.

Less than ten metres now separates me from whatever fate is waiting inside this place. I still can't see anything from here, just a huge pair of dark doors and the steady stream of bodies which go through them. Like so many of the desperate people I've already watched I helplessly glance back over my shoulder. I can't see much but I know there are hundreds and hundreds of people behind me.

There's a sudden noise which takes everyone by surprise. It comes from two directions – from the back end of the queue and also from the other end of the road we were originally queuing along. Even the soldiers appear confused for a second. Many of the troopers surrounding me turn and look back across the field.

It's an attack.

Jesus Christ, someone's attacking from both sides.

In just a few seconds the scene degenerates from resigned calm and relative order into uncontrolled madness. I have no idea who is doing this, but I can see the bright headlights of cars and motorbikes and other random vehicles converging on this building from many directions. They're not just on the road now, I can see them driving across the fields from all around. Fucking hell, this is a coordinated attack.

I stop walking and try and turn back.

'Move, you fucking scum,' a soldier screams at me and I'm hit hard in the middle of the back with something that knocks every scrap of breath out of my body. The force of the impact sends me tripping even deeper into the crowd being pushed through the open doors. I try to resist but I'm struggling to breathe and I can't do anything when more rough arms grab me from either side and throw me forward again. I'm inside now. There's a concrete floor beneath my feet and a high roof over my head which finally shields me from the rain. Behind me the sounds of gunshots and explosions ring out and are suddenly muted as the heavy doors I've just passed through are shut.

It's dark in here and I can hardly see anything. I'm continually pushed and shoved forward until I can't go any further, the mass of bodies in front of me preventing me from moving on. We're tightly packed and it's clear that they've shoved as many of us as they can in here to get us away from whatever it is that's happening outside. The crowd here is silent – unable to move and hardly able to breathe. I can hear a constant soundtrack of muffled shouts, screams and explosions coming from outside.

A sudden crackle of radio static and the soldiers guarding us move again. Up ahead another set of doors is opened, immediately releasing the pressure and allowing the crowd to flood forward into another huge room like water roaring through a suddenly breached dam. I don't want to move but, like everyone else, I have no choice. I know that the deeper I go into this building, the less chance I have of getting out again but there's nothing I can do. I'm carried along by the sheer weight and pressure of everyone else around me and we're all driven forward by the fear of the guns which are constantly aimed at us.

Space.

Unexpectedly I find myself in space and I'm able to move freely. I stop walking and spin around, desperate to try and get my bearings. The light levels in this room are unnervingly low and the people around me are terrified. They're screaming and shouting and yelling for help. I watch helplessly as the doors I've just come through are slammed shut and locked from the inside by more soldiers. These are wearing a different uniform from the others. They're wearing some kind of facemask. Is it a gasmask? It can't be, can it . . . ?

Dead bodies.

My eyes are rapidly becoming accustomed to the low level of yellow light and I can see bodies. Jesus Christ, this room is full of them. They're everywhere – shoved up against the walls, piled up on top of each other around the edges of the room, laid out in lines on the floor . . . my worst suspicions and fears were right. This building is a slaughterhouse. They've brought us here to kill us. They're cataloguing us and destroying us.

I have to get out. I run back towards the closed doors but I'm kicked back into place by one of the masked guards. I've lost all self-control now and I have to fight. I know these soldiers are armed but I don't have any choice and I know I'm dead anyway. I pick myself up and run at the guard again with a speed, strength and determination I didn't know I possessed. I launch myself at him and knock him off his feet before he has time to react. I'm aware of other people starting to fight all around me as I wrestle away his weapon and rip off his mask. He looks up at me with cold, hateful eyes as I punch his face again and again, pounding his flesh with my fists. I continue long after I know he's lost consciousness. I can't stop until I'm sure he's dead . . .

There's a round of gunfire behind me. I spin around and see that one of the other soldiers has opened fire into the crowd. Many have already fallen, the rest of us try and run for cover but there's no-where to hide. In desperation I grab the beaten body of the soldier beneath me and haul it round in front of me like a shield, hoping that it will take the force of any shots that come in my direction.

There are two soldiers firing now. One of them has climbed a metal ladder up onto a galley in the rafters of the building and is picking people out at will. Over the terrified confusion and carnage I can hear another sound now and I look up at the ceiling in terror. It's the chugging of machinery and the hissing of gas. Hanging in the four corners of the room are huge metal boxes with vented fronts which look like air-conditioning units. The air in front of each one of the machines is distorted like a heat haze and I know that it has begun. I throw the corpse off me and start to look around the floor for the mask I tore off its face seconds earlier. The floor in here is awash with blood and bodies and . . .

The world around me explodes.

I drop to the ground and cover my head as the entire far end of the room we're trapped in is ripped apart by a massive blast that sends shrapnel and dead flesh flying in every conceivable direction. Everything becomes black. The noise of the explosion begins to fade and is replaced by yells and screams of pain and fear and by the sounds of a full-scale conflict.

'Run!' a muffled voice yells over the madness and hysteria.

Instinct takes over. I clamber to my feet, tripping and stumbling over rubble and the remains of bodies, and then push my way forward through the clouds of dust and crowds of terrified figures. There is gunfire and confusion all around me. A woman immediately in front of me is shot. For a split second I see blood, flesh and bone explode from her shoulder and she falls to the ground like a limp rag doll. I can't do anything but run straight over her corpse. There's a tide of desperate people moving behind me and I can't stop, I have no option but to keep moving along with the wave of people. I look up and see that we're running towards more soldiers with their guns raised. But these soldiers aren't wearing masks. Their faces and eyes are unprotected and I know immediately that they're on our side. Thank God, these people are on our side.

Still we continue to stumble through the carnage, the ground beneath our feet becoming more uneven and littered with debris. The remains of people like me mix freely with the remains of enemy soldiers. In this grotesque bloodbath they are impossible to separate. No explosion can differentiate between us and them. All around me I can see severed arms and legs, shattered bones and twisted pieces of razor-sharp metal.

'Keep moving,' another voice yells. I feel rain on my face and I realise that I'm outside again, although there are still low mounds of rubble on either side of me which used to be walls. Others have stopped but I keep moving. Another deafening noise distracts me and I look up to see a helicopter roaring low overhead. It unleashes a missile into a long line of trucks which stand idly alongside what's left of the now burning building I've just escaped from. Christ, this is a fucking full-scale war. I sprint across an area of uneven wasteland and throw myself to the ground as more munitions explode nearby. There's a brilliant flash of light to my left and I feel my body being shunted along the ground by the immense force of yet another blast. I'm deafened in one ear and I struggle to regain my balance as I pick myself up and try to move forward again. All around me are the bodies of those who have fallen. A young man's face has taken the full force of the explosion. His lifeless eyes stare up at me helplessly. The bottom of his face, everything below his top lip, has gone. At my feet is the body of a woman, face down in the rubble. Its back is blackened and charred and much of its clothing has been burnt away. It could be Karin, the girl from the queue. For a fraction of a second I think about turning her over to see but I know that it's pointless. It doesn't matter.

In the sky directly above me a second helicopter swoops down and fires into the building I've just escaped from, killing scores of unprotected people who continue to pick their way through the rubble. I manage to take a few more staggering steps away before throwing myself back down again as the first helicopter turns and opens fire on the second. A precisely placed missile hits the middle of its tail boom, taking the rotor clean off and sending the aircraft spiralling down to the ground where it explodes, filling the night with more fire. There is mayhem all around me now, the deafening noise and hysteria of an all-out battle to the death. But who is fighting?

'Get out of here,' a soldier yells, picking people like me up off the ground and pushing them on. I follow the crowd, heading towards an open gate in what's left of the chain-link fence which surrounded this place. Almost as one we run along a gravel track which snakes away into the darkness. Now that we're free we move like a pack, hunting together. The enemy here are few and far between. When we discover them we swarm over them and rip them apart. Behind me the burning building is bathed in light. I look back at it long enough to see hundreds of figures running away from it in every direction.

More soldiers usher us along a track which climbs up into the darkness as another helicopter swoops low overhead. Friend or foe? It's impossible to tell until it launches a volley of missiles into the crowds on the ground. As another ball of flame stretches high up into the sky behind me the sudden increase in light enables me to see my surroundings properly for the first time. The ground below us is littered with an incredible number of bodies. Many of them are victims of the battle now raging but it's clear from their location that many more corpses are those of people like me who have been executed by the others. Their cadavers have been stacked up, ready for disposal. Here alone hundreds of people have been killed. How many other places like this are there, and how many more would have died here tonight? How many of us have been murdered by these bastards, and who are the Haters now?

The top of this low hill now looms ahead of me. I dig in and keep running, my feet slipping and sliding in the greasy mud. I can hear more fighting up ahead and I run towards it, now desperate to be a part of the battle and wanting to take revenge for all the death and destruction I've seen. A few more breathless seconds and I've finally reached the top of the climb. Another huge explosion once again bathes the world in light and I can see a wave of enemy soldiers advancing towards us. Unprotected and without any fear of the consequences I sprint at them. I glance from side to side and see that there are hundreds of people like me moving forward as one. We must destroy them before they can destroy any more of us.

The first of the enemy I reach is firing into the crowd. She has her back to me. Without pausing for thought I leap up onto her back and wrap my arms around her neck. I grab her chin and the back of her head and twist as hard as I can, feeling massive satisfaction as her neck snaps and she crumbles to the ground. In seconds I'm up again, already looking for the next kill. One of them has their weapon aimed directly at me. Before they can fire I run straight at them and charge them down. I move with a speed and power I have never felt before and I feel alive. Faced with death I actually feel more alive! I wrestle the soldier's rifle from his pathetically weak grip and shove its barrel round and hard into his mouth. I fire and watch the top of his head explode into the mud. All around me this animal instinct is taking over and we are killing to keep ourselves alive. This is what I was born to do.

Now another. I rip off a trooper's battle helmet and turn the pathetic creature around to face me. Those eyes. Those fucking eyes glare at me and they are filled with utter hate. I push my thumbs into the sockets and gouge the damn things out, leaving the soldier screaming and writhing on the ground.

All of the confusion and uncertainty has gone. The pain has disappeared. Without fear we fight with unparalleled strength and ferocity. I snap bones and tear flesh and end lives again and again and again.

In the flashes of light and fire which still fill the skies all around here I am able to see the full extent of this battle. It now stretches across a huge expanse of land. It is brutal and relentless, basic and almost medieval. Weapons have been cast aside. This fight is hand to hand – one on one – and our enemy has no answer to our strength and determination. They may have numbers but we have more than that. We have the desire to destroy them and to protect ourselves and others like us. Every one of us will fight with the last breath in our bodies.

Another helicopter rises up in the sky in front of me. I look up and watch as four snaking trails of fire whip across the darkness over my head accompanied by an ear-piercing whistle and a sudden gust of red-hot air. I look back just long enough to see missiles strike the battered and now virtually empty remains of the building we escaped from. There is a momentary pause – like the shortest possible gap between lightning and thunder – followed by the loudest explosion I've yet heard as the hellish place is blasted into a million burning pieces. Even from this distance I can feel the heat of the fire on my skin.

A knife flashes at me from out of nowhere and slices my arm. The adrenaline disguises the pain I feel and I immediately turn on my attacker. He swipes his blade at me again. Somehow I am able to catch his hand midway through its arc. I twist his fist back in on itself and then force the knife round into his own gut. He falls next to the burning shell of an overturned vehicle. Where did I learn to do this? Where did this strength and speed come from? This is instinctive and unstoppable.

'Move out,' a voice screams, barely audible over the confusion. I look up and see that the battle on the hillside is petering out. Although the fighting around what remains of the building below us is continuing, up here on the ridge we have destroyed the enemy. 'Keep moving forward,' the voice instructs. I follow the rest of the crowd as we begin to scramble through the darkness.

43

It's late and out here the world is silent. The noise of battle has long since faded away to nothing. Still surrounded by hordes of others we move quickly through the empty countryside. Armed scouts guide us through the darkness. I don't know where we're going, but I know that I can trust these people and I follow on regardless. I have a feeling in the pit of my stomach which tells me that before long I might finally start getting answers to some of the thousands of questions I've been desperate to ask.

We've marched for more than an hour now and have seen and heard no-one else. Our route has avoided all roads and buildings and virtually all other signs of civilisation. Now we're moving along the base of a deep valley, shielded from view by trees and bushes.

We stop.

'In here,' one of our guides says, ushering us towards a large copse. Without question we move into the trees, stopping only when we've reached the densest part of the woods. The light in here is almost non-existent. One of the scouts kicks around in the undergrowth, seeming to be looking for something. Her foot strikes a small mound in the leaf-covered ground. She bends down and grabs the strap of a bag which one of them must have hidden there previously. She pulls the strap and drags up a large rucksack. Leaves and dirt fall from it as she stands it up and brushes it down. She opens the pack and starts to empty it out.

'Sit down and rest,' one of the other scouts says as his colleague throws packets of food and bottles of water to us. 'Get your strength back,' he continues, 'then listen to the message and leave.'

The message? What message? What's he talking about? I decide that I'll find out later. Right now eating my first food in more than a day is more important than anything else.

I'm sitting with three other people. In the middle of us is a mobile phone, set up ready to play the message. This message, our guides inform us, is as close to the truth as we'll get tonight. It has been distributed as a file by people like us and has spread around the country like a computer virus. It now sits on hundreds of thousands of phones, computers, media players and other devices, too widespread to be deleted.

'Chris who?' a man sitting next to me asks.

'Chris Ankin,' one of the guides replies.

'Who the hell's he?'

'He was a politician,' he explains. 'Used to be fairly high ranking in Defence. He was an adviser to the government when it began. He got to hear a hell of a lot of information before he changed.'

'So where is he now?'

'Rumour has it he's dead.'

'Great.'

'Doesn't matter. He did what he wanted to do before they got him.'

'What was that?'

'He wanted to let us know what was happening. He wanted to warn us. He wanted to try and coordinate us.'

'Coordinate us?'

'Make sure we all know what we have to do.'

'And what's that?'

'Why don't you just play the fucking message?'

The man leans forward and picks up the phone. He struggles with the controls for a second but soon manages to locate the file and starts it playing. At first the words are hard to make out. He adjusts the volume and lifts up the phone so that we can all hear what's being said.

'If you're listening to this,' Ankin's weary voice says, sounding tinny and distorted, 'chances are you don't have a clue what's happened to you or what's happened to the rest of the country. You won't know why you feel the way you do or why your life has just been turned upside down. I'll give you some information but I won't be able to answer all of your questions. I'll tell you what I know but that's not what's important now. Ultimately it doesn't matter why this has happened or what caused it, what matters is how we deal with it. Because of the unprecedented nature of the change and its effects on our society we need to act now and we need to act quickly. There will be time enough to look for reasons when the fight is over.'

I shuffle on the ground and glance at the other faces gathered around the telephone. They stare at the small handset with bewildered expressions. I'm not sure if anyone believes what they're hearing.

'Put simply,' Ankin's voice continues, 'there is a fundamental genetic difference between us and them. A fundamental and basic difference which, until now, has remained dormant. I can't yet tell you why, but something has happened to trigger a change, and that change has created the hate. If you're hoping for me to give you a more scientific explanation, I can't. If you're waiting for me to explain why we can no longer exist alongside the people we loved, lived with and worked with just a couple of weeks ago, I can't. One day we'll understand, but today we don't have the luxury of having either the time or resources to find out.

'Initially it was presumed that the change was limited to just a small minority of people. Before it happened to me, while I was still in office, I saw figures which indicated that our numbers are much greater than was first thought. It's likely that as many as three people in every ten are like us. That's around thirty per cent of the population. That's enough to take the fight to them and stand a chance.

'The change strips away some of the restraint we used to have. In very basic terms it makes us less susceptible to bullshit and more likely to take action. The change seems almost to amplify our instincts. We immediately know who is like us and we know who isn't. We know who poses a threat to us and who is on our side. Many of the layers of conditioning and control imposed upon us by society have been stripped away by the change and no longer apply. Now you fight when you need to fight and you destroy the enemy because you know that they will destroy you if you give them half a chance.

'Until now we've discriminated against each other according to race, religion, age, gender and just about every other differentiation imaginable. Look around you tonight and you'll see that those differences are gone. Now, to put things as simplistically as possible, there is just "us" and "them", and it is impossible for us to coexist. We have no alternative but to fight, and we must keep fighting until we have wiped them out.

'The change has spread across the world with an incredible speed. No corner of the planet has been left untouched. We are everywhere. You must remember that we are not the underdogs. Their advantage over us is in physical numbers only. We have served at every level and among us we have experts in every profession. Among us we have every skill imaginable. We have everything we need to fight them and destroy them.

'Forget your past. Forget your families and friends and who you used to be. In time some kind of normality will be restored. Until then we have no alternative but to fight.'

The message ends and I look at the phone in disbelief. Is this a joke? Can any of this really be true? For a moment I'm overloaded, unable to take it all in. Then my mind begins to fill with memories of the events of the last week and particularly of the last day – the killings, the battles, the bloodshed, the emotions – and I know that every word I've just heard is true. I remember the feelings of strength and power I felt as I killed the enemy soldiers with my hands just a few hours ago and I know that it's all real. Impossible and unproven but real.

SUNDAY

44

The dead politician's words still rattle round my head as I wake up. I've slept for little more than an hour but I feel as refreshed as if I've slept all night. I look up at the canopy of leaves and twisted branches above my head. A familiar face stares back at me.

'Thought it was you,' says Patrick. 'You managed to get away then.'

I sit up quickly. He reaches out his hand and I shake it. I look around and see that many more people have arrived here while I've been asleep.

'You okay?' I ask as I stand up and stretch.

'Absolutely bloody brilliant,' he replies, grinning from ear to ear. 'You?'

I think before answering. In less than twenty-four hours I've lost everything that used to matter to me. I should feel battered, devastated and empty but I don't. I echo Patrick's sentiment. I feel incredible. I feel alive. My body is full of energy and strength. My mind is clear. I'm ready to do what I have to do.

'Never felt like this before,' I tell him. 'I've never felt this good.'

It isn't long before we move on. The scouts who brought us here tell us that there's a small town on the other side of this valley. We'll start there. I know exactly what I have to do. I'm ready now to go into the streets and destroy as many of them as I can find. This battle is only just beginning.

We leave the trees at the bottom of the valley and emerge into a clear and dry morning. The sun is just beginning to rise and I can already hear the sounds of fighting drifting on the breeze. There's a hint of smoke in the air – the smell of their world being torn apart.

Christ, I feel strong. I know now that I've finally thrown off the shackles and restraints of the life I used to lead and I'm free to follow my instincts and do what I was born to do. For the first time since I left her I can think of Ellis this morning and not feel any pain. I know that my little girl is out there somewhere, killing for us. I hope I'll find her again one day. I'll tell her how proud I am.

We move as a pack, powering up the side of the steep hill which looms ahead of us. We reach the top of the climb and I'm barely out of breath. I stand next to Patrick and together we look down onto a truly beautiful scene. In the distance we can see the town, and it is burning. There are already battles raging in the streets. Explosions rock buildings and reduce them to rubble. People are running, fighting and killing.

It's awe-inspiring.

Patrick grins like a child on Christmas morning.

The sun bathes the scene with brilliant, golden light and I can see for miles in every direction. People are swarming towards the town from all sides. With excitement burning in my gut I start to run towards the buildings, desperate to get there, desperate to fight and kill.

We thunder down the other side of the hill, sprint diagonally across a wide and uneven field and then reach the main road into the town. With two others I break into the first building we reach. We smash the front windows of the small, square house and climb in. I find the two elderly occupants upstairs, cowering pathetically in a bedroom. One of them hides under the bed. I grab its foot, drag it out, stand it upright and smash its face into the wall. There's another in the wardrobe. It tries to stay silent but I can hear its unsteady breathing and pitiful whimpering. I pull the doors open, throw it across the room and watch in satisfaction as the other two who are in here with me tear it limb from limb.

By the time we get back outside our bloody attack has been replayed numerous times in numerous houses. Without pausing for breath I run on, desperate to find more of them to destroy.

This is a perfect day.

After so much uncertainty, fear and pain, everything is clear. Everything finally makes sense.

We are at war.